THE RUNAWAY MARTIAN

COZY SCI-FI MYSTERY

KATHERINE OKIA

AGWANG PRESS

First Paperback edition published 2025.

ISBN: 978-1-951722-17-3 eBook

ISBN: 978-1-951722-18-0 Paperback

For my darling daughter, Marta
For my supportive husband, Peter

CONTENTS

CHAPTER 1

Thea strolled through the launch bay of the spaceport in Lunar City, the moon's largest metropolis. A small smile crept across Thea's face as she followed the crowd filing onto the ramp for the space shuttle. Once inside, she selected a seat near a window with a soft chuckle. Pushing her small bag under her chair, she straightened her sage green pants and smoothed her pale yellow shirt as she settled into her seat.

The shuttle had soft, plush beige seats and could hold up to fifty passengers. It was beginning to fill up with families accompanying small children, business passengers, and older adults. Her eyes slid over the other passengers, many of whom were older people. They caught her attention because their final destination was Mars, which would take eight months just one way. She wondered if they were tourists and if this was a once-in-a-lifetime trip for them.

The shuttle sat in a launch tunnel with dimly lit walls, which caused the shuttle's windows to reflect her image. She ran a hand through her shoulder-length auburn hair, trying to straighten out the flyaway strands. She made one large braid down the back of her head and sighed with relief.

Finally, I've escaped, she thought with a lopsided smile.

A few minutes later, after the shuttle's AI had completed the pre-flight checks, it started accelerating through the launch tunnel. After only one or two minutes of acceleration, it burst through the surface of the moon and into the bright sunlight. Thea gazed through the windows with wide eyes as she examined the pitted surface of the moon and then turned to the crescent Earth in the lunar sky. The view of Earth changed periodically through the month, depending on the position of the moon with respect to the Earth and the Sun. She wished she could've stayed in Lunar City for the full month to see how the Earth changed, but she had someplace to be. A moment later, the shuttle made a gentle turn, aiming for a large interplanetary cruiser, the Stargazer, which would become her home for the next eight months.

The star cruiser was covered in gleaming gray metal and adorned with hundreds of little portals that varied in size, depending on the function of the room behind them. The smaller circular windows were usually cabins for the three thousand or so passengers. The larger portals were used for amenities such as the Shopping and Restaurant decks, which included the lobby and was the lowest floor open to passengers. Other facilities included the Games and Entertainment tier, between passenger cabin floors three and four. But the level Thea looked forward to using every day was the Pool and Exercise deck. Above that was the Observation half-floor; the highest level open to passengers that resided above the Exercise portion of that floor.

Thea looked forward to the next eight months. She planned to take advantage of all the ship's relaxing amenities—art classes, spa services, and a daily swim—before she began her job as a farming engineer on Ganymede. Of course, the cruiser wasn't going directly to Ganymede. Instead, it was heading to Anteros, Mars' largest city, and then she would catch a separate ship to Jupiter's moon. But before she had to worry about any of that, she was determined to have fun. It was the first time in years she'd been able to simply relax and be herself.

Several minutes later, the shuttle landed in the Stargazer's launch bay. She heard a rush of air on the shuttle's outside as a force field sealed off the launch bay, and it filled with air. Following the passengers, Thea walked out of the shuttle and down the ramp. Then she waited her turn for the ship's AI to check her in. A small shiver ran down her spine as she hoped her identity documents would pass.

As each passenger stepped through a quick overhead scanner, indicator lights turned from blue to green. This scan verified passengers' identity through facial recognition and their comm bracelets. Comm bracelets verified each citizen's identity. They also used the comms to communicate with each other, receive credits or electronic money for shopping, enjoy entertainment, create businesses, and much more.

Thea held her breath as the number of people between her and the scanner decreased. Finally, it was her turn.

She placed her bag onto a separate conveyor and stepped onto a platform. Her scan beeped and turned from blue to red.

"Ma'am, would you please turn to your left, pick up your bag, and follow the IPS agent," the ship's AI said. Interplanetary Security, or IPS, was the police force for Earth's moon, Mars, Jupiter, and their moons. In addition, they also kept the peace onboard large cruisers like the Stargazer.

"What's the matter?" Thea asked with a slight tremble in her voice.

"Your identity requires additional checks," the AI said.

"What type of additional checks?" Thea asked, shifting from foot-to-foot.

"Ma'am, I can't answer that question," the AI said. "Please step to the left."

Thea stepped off the platform and took her bag. For the first time, she noticed a tall, burly, blond man with a scowl on his face.

"This way, ma'am," the man said, wearing a brown IPS uniform.

"Are you the IPS agent?" Thea asked, trying to keep her voice steady. "I don't understand what this is about."

"Follow me," he said, with a muscle jumping in his jaw.

She followed the IPS agent through another set of doors, down a short hallway, and into a large room where a few more passengers sat at desks as other IPS agents interviewed them.

He grabbed a seat and pressed a button on the table, which caused a floating screen to appear over the surface. The window was dark in the middle as he hadn't asked it to do anything yet, and it had an outline of a pale white light.

"My name is Walker. I just have a few questions for you, and then we'll get you on your way."

What'll I do if this doesn't work? She thought, trying to hide her trembling fingers.

"Are you from Earth?" Walker asked in a bored, flat voice.

"No, I was born in Anteros, Mars," Thea said, squeezing her hands together to stop them from shaking. A moment later, it dawned on her that the IPS should already have all her information. Was this a test?

"How long were you on Earth?" Walker asked.

"Six years," she said. "I was in school at Heliton Academy."

"Heliton? Are you Askov or Askovian?" he asked. About ten percent of the population exhibited special powers that allowed them to move objects with their minds or detect others' thoughts and more. They were called Askovians, and their family members were Askovs.

"I'm Askov, and I have to work to support myself," she said, taking a gamble that they really didn't have all of her information.

Walker nodded and scanned a few more questions on the form.

Thea congratulated herself for telling such a smooth lie. She hated lies, but she had to protect herself. *Why didn't they have my information?*

"I have a niece who goes there, but graduation isn't until tomorrow," Walker said with a raised eyebrow.

"Yes, it's true," Thea said. "I had to miss graduation. I have a job lined up, and I couldn't wait for another ship."

"Is your job in Anteros?"

"No, I'll be working as a farmer in a mining colony on Ganymede."

"How long is your contract?"

"Two years. I am hoping for an extension afterward."

Walker nodded and took another few seconds to scroll through the questions on the floating screen, checking some off and skipping others.

"Alright, it looks like that's all we need," he said, stifling a yawn. "You're free to go."

"Oh, that's it?" she asked with wide eyes.

"Is there more you want to discuss?" Walker said, furrowing his eyebrows.

"No, no, I just wondered why I was pulled out of the line," Thea said.

"It looks as if your information was incomplete," he said, climbing to his feet. "Have you had a problem with your comm before?"

"No," Thea said, examining her teal comm. "It's been fine."

"It's probably nothing," Walker said. "Now, if you'll excuse me, I have to get the next passenger. Just follow the lighting in the floor, and it'll take you to the Stargazer's lobby."

Walker turned and left while Thea gazed at his back before following the lights, gently glowing to guide her. They led her through a narrow hallway up a gently sloping ramp, and when the door slid open, she stood in the gigantic lobby of the Stargazer.

A broad smile covered her face as she stared up at the elaborate set of six chandeliers hanging from the ceiling that looked like translucent shells. Floating robots darted back and forth overhead, helping passengers to find their cabins. The guests chatted among themselves and laughed as they slowly made their way to their cabins. Thea loved the excitement of the patrons on the Stargazer. It felt like the start of a grand adventure, and she couldn't wait.

Before long, a floating robot drifted toward her, asking if she needed help to find her cabin.

"No, I am fine," Thea said, gazing at the spherical robot with the ship's insignia. "My cabin is on the fourth floor, and I know how to get there."

The floating robot darted off to another passenger, and Thea made her way through the lobby to a bank of six antigrav lifts. These lifts worked by altering local gravity around each lift car, allowing it to raise and lower in the shaft. Also, spaceships used alythium to generate localized gravity so that the weight of items and people on the spaceship was the same as the surface of the Earth.

Thea gleefully stepped into the lift and selected the fourth floor. A moment later, the doors opened onto a modern, bright hall with soft carpeting, off-white walls, and softly lit wall sconces around each door. The lighting in the floor indicated she should turn right, so she followed the indicators and gasped when she noticed the view of space at the end of the hall. It was an inky black scene with that wonderful crescent view of the Earth.

Several steps later, the lighting showed her door, room four-one-one. She waved her comm near the door, and it slid open.

"Oh, this is lovely," Thea said as she gazed about the bright room. One large portal dominated a wall, offering a view of space filled with stars. The other walls contained brightly colored stock images.

She laughed as she fell onto the bed and stared at the ceiling.

I can't believe I got away with it.

Thirty minutes later, Thea had showered, dressed, and put on a fresh pale-blue dress. She smoothed down the sides of her dress as she gazed at herself in the mirror. As a tall, gangly woman, she loved any dress that emphasized her meager curves. Pursing her lips, she wished for the thousandth time that she'd been born with a body like her sister's, but she shook her head.

That's my old life, she thought.

She turned to the bathroom counter and stretched out her arm. As Thea used her Mover abilities, an unusual translucent teal-colored bracelet floated through the air and slid over her left hand, stopping at her wrist. Now that she had started her journey to Anteros, she thought of the person who had given her the teal comm and what could have been. Then her chest slightly tightened as she remembered the tiny white lie she'd told Agent Walker when they discussed the comm. She wasn't an Askov but a fully trained Askovian.

Several minutes later, she roamed the Shopping floor as a light, bubbly feeling filled her chest. She stopped at a crystal boutique and studied the multicolored figurines in the window, wondering if she could recreate the colors on her screen. As she walked further along the floor, she passed a candle store and several other specialty shops. After exploring for a while, she headed up to the Restaurant mezzanine.

One of the first doors on this floor led to a Martian eatery. She wrinkled her nose as she knew she'd be eating a lot of Martian food when she reached Mars. Also, Martian food made by non-Martians didn't taste the same as the food from her childhood. She continued further down the walkway, pausing as she passed a coffee café with pastries, but decided she wanted a proper meal. After a few more steps, she found what she was looking for: a steakhouse.

Stepping inside, she inhaled the fantastic smell of freshly cooked steak as the corners of her mouth twitched. She took in the dark, rich colors, elegant decor, and the cozy, secluded tables. Couples gathered at most of the tables, which would normally leave her feeling nostalgic for the past. Today, she didn't care; she was simply hungry.

An orange and black robot floated toward her.

"How many will be joining you?" the floating spherical robot asked.

"It's just me," Thea said with a gleeful smile.

"Please follow me," the robot said, turning mid-air and following a series of walkways toward the back of the restaurant.

"Will this table be alright?" the robot asked.

"Yes, it's perfect," Thea said with a broad smile as she took her seat.

Her table gave her a view of the entire dining area. It was decorated with a screen showing a nighttime view of a forest on Earth. Unobtrusive floating sound dampeners hung between each table, muting everyone's voices. There was something very calming about the steakhouse, and she took a deep breath, feeling the tension ease from her shoulders.

Looking at the meal crafter's menu, she ordered a steak with potatoes and crystallized asparagus. This device connected to a hidden pantry that created fully prepared meals and teleported them to the table.

Steak was one of her favorite meals she discovered in her six years on Earth. She also loved the crunchiness of the crystallized vegetables and especially liked the way asparagus tasted with steak.

The steak was actually synthetic because it was grown in a lab from the cells of a cow, but it tasted exactly how a steak should taste. Even though steak was common in all human colonies, it was never prepared the same way. Also, crystallized vegetable preparation was only available on Earth and Lunar City.

A moment later, her entire meal materialized on the table.

"Mmm..." she said as she inhaled.

She chewed on the first bite of her steak and savored the juicy meat.

Either I am hungry, or that's the best steak I've ever had, she thought.

She continued with the second bite and then moved to the crystallized asparagus. The first crunch set off an explosion of flavor combined with the crunchiness that created an amazing food experience. She remembered why this was her favorite meal and worked her way through the asparagus, the steak, and the mashed potatoes.

After she finished her meal and had the credits deducted from her account, she continued her stroll through the gallery of restaurants before heading back to her cabin. She noticed that some started to close. The Stargazer kept a twenty-four-hour day, and most businesses closed in the late evening.

A slight frown played on her lips as she thought about the talk with her parents two months earlier. She had tried to speak to her parents one last time about her job choices, where she lived, and who she spent time with. It hadn't gone well, and after that, she'd given up.

Her last week of school had flown by in a big rush as she prepared for her new life as a farming engineer. She had sold most of her belongings, said an early goodbye to some close friends, and evaded a couple of cousins who attended Heliton with her. She'd never been close to them and didn't think they would mind, as they avoided her, too.

In the early morning hours, she had sneaked out of her dorm room, traveled to the spaceport, and boarded the shuttle from Earth to Lunar City. After arriving in Lunar City, she caught a second shuttle to the Stargazer ship. A moment of guilt settled in her chest as she reflected on the fight she'd had with her parents, but since they wouldn't listen, a clean break was best for everyone.

It had been a long day, and she felt its heaviness on her shoulders. After taking a deep breath, she turned, heading for her cabin.

"Fourth floor," Thea said as she stepped onto the antigrav lift, which began to move. She exhaled, feeling more heaviness settle onto her body, and leaned against one wall of the lift. A moment later, she heard a giant crash immediately above her, and suddenly a woman's body fell through the lift's ceiling and thumped onto the floor.

Thea screamed.

CHAPTER 2

After a few seconds, Thea pulled herself together, and her mind began frantically looking for a solution. She considered touching the woman's neck to see if her heart was still beating, but judging by its funny angle, she knew that couldn't be true.

Why was the lift still moving? The emergency safeties should've activated and stopped her car.

"Help, help, somebody's injured here!" Thea said in shallow breaths, eyes wide.

The AI, which normally assisted her in the antigrav lift, didn't respond. Even though that was odd, Thea didn't have time to reflect on it. Instead, she activated her bracelet with a frantic touch.

"Please help; somebody's been injured," Thea yelled.

"What is the nature of your emergency?" a mechanical-sounding AI replied.

"There's a woman in the lift, and I think she's dead," Thea said.

"Have you activated the medipad in the lift?" the AI asked. The medipad was an oval floating device that could fold flat to create a gurney while providing medical care.

"No, where is it?" she asked, quickly glancing around the small space. Just as she spotted the button, the AI replied.

"Look for a large red button labeled 'Emergency.' Once you select it, the medipad will activate," the AI said. "I have sent two IPS agents, and they will meet you on the fourth floor where your lift has stopped."

"Why won't the doors open?" Thea asked, taking careful steps around the body.

"Unknown," the AI replied. "I've relayed that information to the IPS."

After pressing the emergency button multiple times, she replied, "Nothing's happening; the medipad won't activate."

"Please wait patiently. The door to your lift has malfunctioned. The maintenance robots are currently working to open your lift, and more IPS agents have deployed to assist you."

Thea turned and examined the woman from the other side of the lift. Her neck was clearly broken, but a strange thought crossed her mind. The woman was stunningly beautiful. She must've been an Askov or Askovian.

"Thea Black," a loud voice called from the other side of the lift doors. "Can you hear me?"

"Yes, yes, I'm here," Thea shouted. "Please open the doors."

"We're working on it," the voice said. "We have a couple of robots here that are trying to force the doors open. Are you injured?"

"No, I am fine," Thea said, glancing at the woman as tightness gripped her chest.

"Please be patient," the voice said. "I'm Agent Walker. Do you remember me?"

"Yes, I remember," Thea said, desperately trying to hold on to her panic.

"This is important," Walker said. "Touch as little as possible in the lift. We'll need to perform a forensic sweep. Understand?"

"Of course," she said. "I won't touch anything."

A few minutes later, the doors to the lift slid open, and Thea stumbled out and crashed into a woman wearing a brown uniform. She gazed at the woman for a moment and realized she was looking at an IPS agent.

"Thea Black?" the IPS agent asked. Her brown hair was in a tight ponytail.

Thea nodded as her whole body trembled.

"Please step this way," the agent said, gently guiding Thea with a half-hug. "We'll give them some room to examine the body."

Thea walked with the agent, who supported her with an arm around her shoulders. Normally, Thea didn't like being so close to strangers, but right now, the embrace steadied her nerves. They walked just a few steps down the hall of the fourth floor. The agent selected a medipad from the wall and helped Thea onto it.

"I don't really need medical care," Thea said.

"I'm Agent Clark, by the way," she said. "Just in case, I thought you could sit for a quick medical scan."

Thea sighed and glanced at the door to the lift. The victim lay on a second medipad. Thea gawked at the woman's beauty; her thick, long blonde hair, high cheekbones, and perfectly symmetrical face. *Definitely an augmented Askov or Askovian,* she thought. There was a trend among Askov families to genetically alter their kids to become their ideal of perfection: flawless skin, silky hair, completely symmetrical, tall, and slender.

The victim's neck remained at its funny angle, and she finally noticed the woman wore a long, pale green dress and looked as if she was heading to a party or some sort of event. Thea wondered how the woman had fallen through the roof of a lift. It should be impossible to even get into the shafts that housed the lifts.

"I know this must be upsetting, especially if you've never seen a dead body before," Agent Clark said. "Did you know the victim?"

Thea shook her head, even though there was something familiar about her flawless features. She wondered what event the woman had attended or was on her way to.

"Our records show that you're an Askov, and we simply wondered if you might know who she is," Clark said.

"No, what was her name?" Thea asked.

"Veronica Dover," the agent said. "She also attended Heliton Academy. But she graduated ten years earlier. We thought you might know one of her relatives."

"I went to school with a couple of Dovers," Thea said. "But she doesn't look like any of them."

"Thank you," Clark said. "The medipad is recommending a mild sedative."

Clark handed Thea a small bottle synthesized by the medipad.

Thea shook her head. "I don't want to take anything. I just need to get out of here. When can I go?"

"I'm not in charge of this investigation. We have to wait for Agent Walker. He may have more questions for you."

"Walker?" Thea asked. "I thought he was a customs agent."

"IPS agents making the transit to Mars are always required to perform multiple duties," Clark said. "One of them is customs. We also act as the onboard security for the ship, as there are around three thousand people here."

They waited quietly for a few minutes when two more people arrived in navy blue uniforms and approached her.

"Ms. Thea Black?" the older gentleman with white hair and bronze skin asked. He nodded his greeting. "I'm Captain Ebert, and this is Commander Gotham. We're so sorry for the shock you must've experienced. We'd like to extend our humblest apologies."

Thea nodded to both men but couldn't think of a reply.

"While this investigation is ongoing, we'd like to ask you not to mention this to any of the other passengers," Captain Ebert said.

"Of course," Thea said, repressing a shiver.

Strangely, even though she didn't recognize the victim at all, there was something familiar about Commander Gotham. He was shorter than the captain, with close-cropped, brown hair and striking green eyes. She felt they might have met a long time ago—maybe even when she was a child, but she couldn't quite place him.

She watched as a new woman in a navy blue uniform stepped from around the corner. She was an energetic woman who bounced on her feet as she walked and wore her hair in a single braid down her back.

"Dr. Hadley," the captain said, following her into the lift.

Thea couldn't hear any more of their conversation.

Twenty minutes later, she endured a brief exam with Dr. Hadley, who offered a sedative. Thea refused. This was followed by a round of questioning by Agent Walker. Afterward, she headed seven doors down the hall to her cabin.

Agitated from today's event, she paced her room, wondering if she should have taken that mild sedative. Instead, she decided to take a hot bath.

Several minutes later, she slid into the warm, soapy water, laid back, and relaxed. In moments, she began to feel the tension easing out of her body as she closed her eyes.

Thea's mind kept wandering over the dead woman. What was she like when she was alive? Who was her family? She felt sorry for Veronica Dover, who had died so young. Strangely, she didn't look like any of the Dovers, who tended to have an olive complexion and black hair.

Then she wondered about the commander. Why did he seem so familiar? Suddenly, her eyes popped open. Samuel Gotham. She vaguely remembered he had a sister, Jemma, who was friends with Thea's older sister, Mara.

Because of a ten-year age gap, Thea rarely spent time with her older siblings or their friends. But she recalled seeing Samuel a few times. She wondered why he never acknowledged her—maybe he didn't remember her.

Both of Thea's siblings considered her inferior because they had been augmented, whereas she was not. Thea's parents had tried to alter her, too. But the process had nearly killed her, and the doctors had to abandon it.

Samuel and his sister were not augmented, but her mom and siblings had accepted them, anyway. Her old feelings of rejection and not fitting in resurfaced, but then she remembered that she had already made plans to escape that world. She was going to start a new job among people who would not judge her for being ordinary.

CHAPTER 3

After hiding in her room all day, Thea finally decided to leave her cabin the following evening. She tried to recover from the shock of witnessing the woman falling to her death right before her. But after several hours of brooding on it, Thea forced herself to embrace the world again. She showered and changed into her favorite clothing, a soft, cream-colored, comfortable, long-sleeved dress.

She made her way to the bank of lifts and shivered as she passed the lift where she had encountered the dead woman. Noticing it was closed, she took another lift to the bottom floor, then took the stairs to a mezzanine. Multiple restaurants jammed together filled this partial floor, and one in particular caught her interest.

It was a vegetarian eatery featuring all crystallized vegetables. She had been looking forward to this, as it was one of the top-rated ones on the ship because of its use of unusual seasonings. As she stepped inside, she paused in the lobby area, waiting for a floating robot to seat her. A moment later, a human appeared, which caused her to raise an eyebrow.

"How many will be joining you this evening?" the waiter asked in a low, discreet voice.

"Uhmm...sorry, I'm just so surprised. I was expecting a robot," Thea said with a wry smile. Only very high-end services use human staff for a customized experience like real estate rentals, vacations, and fine dining.

"It's one hallmark of our commitment to an excellent patron experience," the server said, maintaining his composure. "Where possible, we include as much of the human touch to create a personalized experience for our guests."

Thea thought this sounded like some sort of commercial, but she was hungry and simply nodded.

"It's just me," she said.

"Right this way," the host said, gesturing for her to follow him.

A moment later, the waiter seated her at a table right in the middle of the dining area. However, it was surprisingly quiet, and she looked up to find the floating sound dampeners. Reaching for the meal crafter, she scrolled, trying to choose a meal among the twenty or so listed. After a while, she chose one labeled veggie steak. She briefly wondered what that could be but decided today was a good day to be adventurous. She made her selection, and a moment later, a glass of wine materialized on her table.

Taking a deep breath, she peered at the other guests. The lighting was low, and there was a lot of privacy between each table due to the strategic placement of plants. A moment later, her meal materialized on the table.

Of course, it looked nothing like a steak, but it smelled delicious. She looked at a pile of mashed potatoes and tasted it with her fork. It was soft, creamy, and perfectly seasoned. She stuck her fork into something that could have been a mushroom, but she wasn't sure. Deciding to try it, she cut off a slice and chewed.

"Mmm...I've never tasted something so good," Thea said, then quickly glanced around, hoping nobody heard her. The taste was meaty, even though she was sure she was eating a mushroom. It had been seasoned exactly the way one might expect a steak to be seasoned, but the mushroom had a way of feeling very satisfying once it landed in her stomach. Even though she only intended to have a bite, she continued carving more pieces off and chewing. This was the best meal she'd had on board yet.

Several minutes later, after she finished the whole mushroom, a man walked near her table and stopped.

"What are you doing here?" the man said, glaring at Thea. He had black, wavy hair and an olive complexion.

She paused with the fork halfway to her mouth and stared at him wide-eyed.

"Why aren't you in jail?" the black-haired man said more aggressively, taking a step toward her.

"I'm sorry. Do I know you?" Thea asked, wondering if someone was playing a cruel joke on her.

"You know damn well who I am," he said. "You just murdered my wife."

Thea paused with her mouth open, nonplussed.

"Get out of here," the black-haired man said, now leaning on her table and hovering over her.

"Owen, what's the matter?" A woman with dark hair and an olive complexion joined him at the table. "I think you're making a scene. Leave her alone."

Then it finally hit Thea. She was looking at one of the Dover family members. He must have been the husband of that poor, dead woman.

"I don't understand. Why do you think I killed your wife?" Thea said, trying to make sense of his words.

"We've seen the evidence from the IPS," Owen said. "We know you did it."

"The IPS told us not to confront her," the woman said. "They're doing their own inquiries, and you may have messed that up."

"Quiet, Lottie," Owen said, glaring at her. "It wasn't your spouse murdered in cold blood." He turned back to Thea. "What I want to know is why you aren't in jail."

"I'm sorry, but I really don't know what you're talking about," Thea said. "Why would I be in jail? I was standing in the lift by myself when suddenly a woman's body came through the ceiling and crashed onto the floor. There's no way I could've killed her if I was already in the lift."

"That's not what we heard from the IPS," Owen said.

"Come on now," Lottie said, dragging on Owen's arm as hard as possible. "They said not to talk to her. You could be messing up their work. Come." She dragged again, but he refused to budge from the table.

"Is there a problem here?" the waiter reappeared, glaring at Owen.

"She should be in prison for murdering my wife," Owen said, pointing a finger at Thea.

Thea opened her mouth to reply, but the server interrupted her.

"Sir, I'm going to have to ask you to leave. You're disturbing the other guests," the host said.

"Come along, Owen. You've caused enough trouble. Come now," Lottie said, yanking harder on Owen's arm.

"You haven't heard the last of this," Owen said, his face contorted with anger. "I'm going to have you put in jail."

Lottie continued dragging him, and eventually, they left the restaurant.

"I'm very sorry for this disturbance," the waiter said to her. "We'd like to offer a free dessert. Anything that you'd like?"

Thea breathed a sigh of relief while trying to make sense of her jumbled thoughts.

What was going on? she thought.

"I'm sorry, but I've lost my appetite," Thea said. "Would you box this up for me and send it to my room?"

"Better than that, in the following days, if you want to have a meal here or in your room, we'll provide it free of charge," the waiter said. "We apologize for any inconvenience."

"Thank you," Thea said, carefully scanning her surroundings as several people stared at her. She simply wanted to leave. Standing, she nodded to the server and made her way to the exit.

She considered returning to her cabin, but she'd been cooped up there all day. Instead, she decided to roam through the Restaurant mezzanine to the lifts and ended up just above the third passenger cabin floor, the Games and Entertainment deck.

It was later in the evening as the ship maintained a twenty-four-hour day. Strolling past several casinos, floor games like Space Puck, and a mini auditorium. She returned to the lift and ended at the second-highest passenger deck, the Pool and Exercise deck.

She stepped off the lift while her eyes roamed the broad walkway in front. To her left was the exercise area, but she was interested in the water to the right. There was a huge glass ceiling covering four pools. A giant water slide crowned the one intended for kids, and it was closed. But she heard muted chatter from the adults in the remaining three. Glancing through the ceiling, she grinned at the dramatic view of the pitch-black vacuum dotted with thousands of tiny stars.

Continuing her amble, she passed a few health spas and gyms. Most were closed, but she didn't care. She just needed something to do while she filtered through what had just happened at the restaurant.

Why did he think I killed his wife? she thought.

She considered reaching out to Agent Walker, but considering the hour, Thea decided maybe she'd rethink who to contact tomorrow morning after she'd had a good night's sleep.

At least one thing became clear: Veronica Dover didn't look like the other Dovers because she had married into the family. The Dovers were generally Movers, just like Thea's family. She had hoped to escape that world, as most of them tended to stay in Anteros. But she should've known she couldn't completely hide, and now she might have to deal with something far more serious.

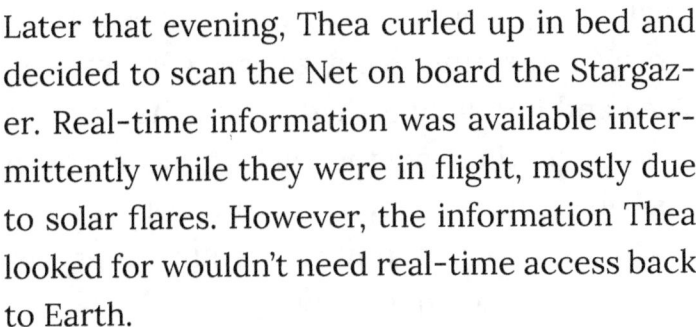

Later that evening, Thea curled up in bed and decided to scan the Net on board the Stargazer. Real-time information was available intermittently while they were in flight, mostly due to solar flares. However, the information Thea looked for wouldn't need real-time access back to Earth.

Thea selected her comm, creating a floating screen with a dark middle and a pale white light outline. "Please show me the family tree of the Dover family, starting with the oldest living family member."

A second later, an entire family tree appeared.

"Larger than I expected," Thea said, using her fingers to shift the chart around so she could see all the family members. Moments later, she found Owen Dover. He was listed as being married to Veronica. She was an Abbot who were also Movers. In the Askov world, a marriage between two families with abilities was seen as a good match.

Owen was in his early thirties and at a similar age to Thea's brother and sister. Although Thea hadn't heard her siblings mention Owen and Lottie, she was sure they would've been at least acquaintances and probably friends given the small number of Askovs and Askovians on Anteros. On the other hand, the age gap between Thea and her siblings had meant they almost never spent time together. In fact, she had been the baby to fix her parents' marriage. It had sort of worked as her parents stayed together, but they were clearly not happy.

It turned out Lottie was his younger sister by about two years. She seemed to be the level-headed one. But to be fair, he's probably distraught at the loss of his wife.

Tomorrow, she'd have to ask Agent Walker why the Dovers think she killed Veronica.

CHAPTER 4

Early the following morning, Thea drifted in and out of consciousness as a chime periodically disrupted her sleep. Groaning, she realized the sound came from her comm. She rolled over on her bed and glared at her blue-tinted bracelet for a moment before launching the vidchat.

"Thea Black?" Agent Walker asked as his image appeared on a floating window above her comm.

"Yes," Thea said in a croaky voice. "Why are you calling so early?"

"It's not really that early," the agent said. "It's ten in the morning. Do you need some time to wake up?"

"No, it's okay," Thea said, pulling herself upright in her bed. "What do you want?"

"We'd like to question you a little further about the murder of Veronica Dover," Walker said.

"More questions?" she asked. "But I don't have anything else to add."

"We just have a few follow-up questions. It'll only take a few minutes. Can you come down in about an hour?" the agent said.

"Well...I've been meaning to talk to you about something," she said as sleepiness faded from her mind. "Yesterday, I had an encounter with somebody. I think his name was Owen Dover."

"Yes, we heard all about that last night," Walker said. "It's the reason we want to talk to you today. We specifically asked him not to contact you, but it seems that now news of the murder has spread throughout the ship. Anyway, we have a few more follow-up questions, but like I said, this won't take long."

"Very well," Thea said and sighed. "I'll be there in about an hour."

An hour and a half later, Thea made her way to a bank of lifts she'd never noticed before. These lifts took the crew and IPS agents to three restricted floors of the ship. Today, her bracelet gave her permission to go there as well. She took the antigrav lift to the sixth floor. As she stepped off, she looked at what seemed like an endless maze of walls and hallways. The walls were all the same shade of gray, with the flooring being darker and the ceiling white. It wasn't even broken up with wall paintings or plants or anything. She wrinkled her eyebrows in confusion.

"Thea Black," an AI voice said. "Please follow the lighting in the floor." It sprang to life, indicating the direction. "You are going to conference room six-one-B."

Thea followed the lighting through the maze of hallways. After the first couple of left and right turns, she had no idea where she was on the ship. She walked past several more doors when the hall ended with a set of double doors. They slid apart, revealing two IPS agents in brown uniforms.

"Ms. Black, please come in," Agent Walker said with a gesture, his blond hair perfectly arranged. He sat on the long side of a rectangular table next to a small floating screen.

Thea stepped inside, and her eyes slid over more gray walls. She nodded to Agents Walker and Clark, who sat beside one another. Thea took a seat across from them with her back to the door.

"I'm sorry to have to call you here," Walker said. "But we needed to talk to you about the death of Veronica Dover, as something fairly serious has come up."

"What is it?" Thea asked as she shifted in her seat, wondering again if they'd discovered her secret.

Agent Walker turned to Clark.

"Take a moment to look at the screen," Agent Clark said as she selected something on her small floating window. A moment later, a large image appeared at one end of the table. A few minutes later, the screen started a vid.

"Why do you have a vid of me at a restaurant?" Thea asked, inclining her head.

"Trust me, this is important," Clark said. "I'll just play a little bit of it because, obviously, you were there. This happened during the time we think Ms. Dover was murdered."

Thea watched herself eat for several seconds, wondering if she was supposed to be observing something else. She noticed some of the other patrons around, but there was nothing unusual about them. Then Agent Clark sped the vid up a few times just to show the time.

"Now, I'd like you to take a look at this vid," Clark said.

Observing herself strolling along the Restaurant mezzanine, her image periodically stopped to look into the windows of various eateries. She wondered again, if she was supposed to pay attention to the specific businesses or the people walking by, but nothing struck her as unusual.

"Pay attention to the time as you go to the lifts," Clark said.

Eying herself as she stepped into the lifts, Thea squeezed her eyes closed, but she still heard the sound of Ms. Dover's body crashing through the roof.

"The reason we're showing you these vids is they completely conflict with some other data we have," Agent Walker said.

They all turned back to the large screen, and this time, Thea saw a moving dot leave her cabin at the same time that she ate on the first-floor mezzanine.

"This blue indicator appears to be you," Agent Clark said. "It has the same signal as your bracelet."

"I don't understand," Thea said. "How's that even possible? Shouldn't there have been an alarm or something?"

"We're still looking into that," Walker said. "For some reason, our local Net doesn't mind having two instances of the same person. We think it's a recent bug. Our system was over-hauled a few weeks ago."

He nodded to Clark, who continued.

"Here, you leave your cabin, go up to the fifth floor, and into the Dovers' cabin," Clark said. "This green indicator is Ms. Dover. Something happens inside the cabin."

"We don't have cams inside each cabin unless needed," Walker explained.

"Watch as both the green and blue signals head to the lifts, and the green shape heads down the shaft," Clark said. "The problem here is there's no way to open the entrances to those shafts unless you're actually inside the lift, so how did you do that?"

"How did I do what?" Thea asked in a raised voice, afraid they were accusing her of murder. "I obviously wasn't there."

"Yes, we know," Walker said. "We've seen you on the vids at the same time the murder was committed. What we don't understand is why your bracelet has the same signature as the killer's."

"Are you expecting me to explain that?" Thea asked with a smirk. "I obviously don't know."

"Did you receive a comm replacement recently?" Clark asked.

"Uhmm..." Thea hesitated, needing a good lie. "I broke it earlier this year and got a new one, but I don't see what that has to do with anything."

Thea cleared her throat, fighting to keep her nerves under control and hoping they hadn't seen through that lie. She maintained a neutral face as much as possible.

Agents Walker and Clark didn't seem to notice; instead, both took notes on their floating screens.

"There's a chance someone stole your identity, maybe when you got your new comm," Agent Walker said. "But if so, why wait so long to start using the new bracelet?"

"Have you had any other issues with this bracelet?" Agent Clark asked. "Any issues with purchases appearing on your ledger?"

"No, nothing at all," Thea said, trying to repress a shudder. "I check my ledger routinely, and I've never had an issue using the bracelet anywhere. But why would someone use my comm's signal?"

"It's possible somebody stole your identity information here on the ship," Walker said. "But it's highly unlikely. We have much higher security here on an interplanetary ship."

"Is that why Owen Dover thinks I killed his wife?" Thea asked.

"Yes, I'm afraid so," Walker said. "Someone talked to Mr. Dover."

"It was a good lesson for us," Clark said, exchanging a look with Walker.

"We'll be careful about releasing information to the crew," Walker said. "We've talked to Mr. Dover and his sister again and asked them both not to approach you."

"If you have trouble with either one, please let us know immediately," Clark said. "We'll confine one or both of them."

"One more thing," Thea said as a thought crossed her mind. "Why was Veronica dressed for a party?"

"Ah..." Clark turned to Walker.

"There was a small get-together planned for that evening," Walker said. "It's a tradition among the crew to hold a small launch party for themselves and any significant others. They canceled at the last minute due to a small emergency."

"I suppose Veronica may not have changed yet," Thea said.

Later that afternoon, Thea stepped to the edge of the water on the Pool and Exercise Deck. Taking in the sparkling blue water, she inhaled the water's mildly metallic smell, which reminded her of childhood and spending endless hours in the water. Muted chatter of the sparse swimmers surrounded her, adding to her nostalgia. The lighting, set to a sunny day, masked most of the inky view of space with a smattering of stars. With a small smile, she jumped in.

The water enveloped her, leaving her skin feeling tingly. She kept her eyes open as she liked the way the water distorted pool toys and other swimmers. Holding her breath underwater, she swam closer to the bottom of the pool. After a moment, when she felt she couldn't hold her breath any longer, Thea bobbed to the surface and exhaled as a brilliant smile covered her face, and she laughed. She hadn't been swimming in months, and the experience felt wonderful, as if all the troubles of the previous days had just washed away.

She continued swimming in the water, turning on her back for the backstroke, rearranging herself for the sidestroke, and generally goofing around. After about twenty or thirty minutes of swimming, she made her way back to her lounge chair.

Using her towel, she dried off instead of the mini dryers dotted around the pool area because she knew she was going back in. After reclining on a lounge chair, she sipped on a cold, fruity drink that was a combination of pineapple, coconut, and mango. The tropical taste left her smiling as she took in the pool and swimmers when a shadow fell over her.

"Dorathea Romly?" a woman said, dressed in a black swimsuit with her thick black hair tied back in a ponytail. She held a bag full of belongings with a towel halfway hanging out. "Call me Lottie. Should I call you Dora?"

Thea froze. She hadn't heard her childhood name for years. Slowly turning her head, she stared wide-eyed at Lottie and immediately recognized the similarities to her brother Owen.

Lottie smiled hesitantly, walking to the lounge chair on the other side of the small table next to Thea's lounge.

"I know the IPS asked me and Owen not to bother you," she faltered. "But I want you to know this is all genuine. There are cams in here, and if you don't feel comfortable around me, you can call for the IPS anytime."

"What do you want?" Thea asked as her eyes narrowed.

"First, I want to apologize for my brother," Lottie said. "He should've never approached you in that restaurant. And I'm sorry that you didn't get a chance to enjoy the rest of your meal. But really, what he said was the most damaging of all—accusing you of murder when there's no evidence that points to you at all. In my opinion, you seem to be a victim just like Veronica."

Thea's shoulders relaxed a little; she hadn't expected any sort of apology from Lottie.

"Well...I suppose you're not the one who needs to apologize," Thea said. "But thank you anyway."

"I know. I'm really apologizing for my brother," Lottie said. "He's not likely to apologize anytime soon. He's..."

"Grieving," Thea said, finishing her sentence. "I'm sure he must be upset."

"There's another reason I want to talk to you, Dora," Lottie said. "Why are you going by a different name now?"

Thea sighed and turned to the pool to think. She knew this day was coming, but she had thought she would at least make it to Anteros. For some reason, she decided to be honest with Lottie.

"I haven't used Dora for six years now," Thea said, pursing her lips. "It's Thea. How did you know it was me?"

"I'd know you anywhere, Thea," Lottie said with a gentle smile. "You're the spitting image of your mother, and you even have the same auburn hair. Our moms were best friends, so I saw her all the time. But I don't think you spent much time at our house."

Thea shook her head as she remembered the number of times she'd been excluded from many of those outings with other Askov families. It was as if her mother was ashamed of her. But that didn't make sense since she looked almost exactly like her mom.

"I hope you don't call the IPS because I would like to get to know you," Lottie said. "Soooo, why are you Thea Black?"

Thea realized Lottie knew a lot about her already. Remaining quiet, she turned from Lottie to the water. She saw a few couples casually swimming, but mostly, they stopped and chatted with each other. On the other side of the deck, she could hear the children in the larger pool screaming and splashing. And through this, she just wondered how much she could trust Lottie.

"I have an idea," Lottie said. "You've just recently met me. You don't have to tell me anything right now. Why don't we just become friends first?"

Thea turned to face her. "Are you going to tell anyone about my name?"

"No, not even my brother," Lottie said with a sly smile. "Can we become friends?"

Thea nodded slowly.

"Good, I'm happy you've agreed," Lottie said with a bright smile. "I hope this is the beginning of a wonderful friendship." She paused for a moment and frowned. "You know, anytime you don't want to continue our friendship, just be honest. I know this is a little awkward for you and also for me. But I've always wondered why your mom never brought you around, even though we knew of you."

Lottie leaned closer with a playful smile. "You know, I have a secret."

"What is it?" Thea said, drawn into Lottie's bubbly tone.

Lottie glanced around the Pool deck as if looking for eavesdroppers. "I'm going to investigate Veronica's murder."

Thea gasped.

"I want you to help me," Lottie said, giggling.

"No," Thea said with a firm shake of her head.

"Just hear me out," Lottie said. "I've heard lots of rumors about the IPS not taking Askov interests seriously. They're more likely to help Originals. I just think with my connections into the Askov world, I could find more clues." Originals was a slang term used to refer to humans with no ties to an Askov family and no special abilities.

"You didn't have a dead body fall to your feet," Thea said with a shiver. "Absolutely not. It's too dangerous."

Lottie shrugged a shoulder and took a sip of her drink. Thea turned back to the water, wondering if Lottie was reckless or simply not too smart.

CHAPTER 5

T he following afternoon, Thea sat on a tall stool in a painting class, hunched over a floating electronic canvas as she added light strokes to outline her image. The class's structure offered instructions from a spherical floating robot in the first half and passenger painting in the second. Thea had been creating colorful compositions for over half her life and didn't think she could learn anything from a cruise ship art class. But she had joined Lottie and a new friend for their company. She analyzed her sketch as she considered the best way to display the vase at the center of the class.

"Don't you think this is so much fun?" Lottie said with a small smile. "I haven't taken a painting class since I was a kid." She adjusted her digital floating canvas and compared her drawings to the vase in the center of the room.

Lottie introduced Thea to Jemma just before the start of the class. Even though Thea'd never met Jemma, she remembered Lottie and Jemma had been friends with Thea's sister, Mara. Thea had recently seen those unusual green eyes—Sam Gotham. Obviously, they were siblings. The Gothams hadn't augmented their children to resemble the Askov's beauty ideal. This further confirmed they had limited assets and income. Lottie and Jemma were about ten years older than Thea.

"I took a couple when I was in school," Jemma said with a smirk. Her lack of painting experience showed in the sloppy application of blue coloring to her floating window. "But I was trying to avoid math classes."

Lottie and Jemma giggled but then returned to their floating canvases and continued filling in their sketches of the vase at the center of the room.

Thea decided to add more decoration to her vase, transforming it from a modern-day container to something that may have been more suitable in an ancient temple.

"What about you, Thea?" Lottie asked. "Did you like math in school?"

"It was okay," Thea said. "Just not my favorite subject. I took a huge number of painting classes, too."

"Well, I can tell those classes paid off," Jemma said with a lopsided smile. "Your vase looks significantly better than everybody else in the class."

Thea muttered a thank you while turning pink; she peeked at the other students before returning to her own canvas.

The three women stood in a U-shape at one corner of the class, which made them a little separate from everyone else.

"So, has Lottie told you about her new lark?" Jemma asked in a loud whisper. "She's going to figure out who killed poor Veronica before the IPS."

Thea paused and stared at her, nonplussed, before going back to her canvas.

"She doesn't really approve of my fun," Lottie said with an exaggerated frown to Jemma. "I'm not going to do anything to interfere with their investigation. Instead, I'll ask a few questions among friends and see what I can find out."

"Well, I think it's brilliant and loads of fun," Jemma said. "I can't wait to get started. Who will be your first target?"

"I'm not sure," Lottie said. "Even though I haven't given it much thought yet, I was thinking of gathering intel at the daily afternoon teas."

"Perfect," Jemma said. "The old biddies are such gossips. If there's anything to be dug up, they'll know it."

"Don't you think that's perfectly safe?" Lottie asked Thea.

"I suppose." Thea shrugged. "Who're the old biddies?"

Lottie and Jemma tittered.

"They're Askovs who like to act like everyone's grandma," Lottie said. "But really, they're nosy busybodies."

"But they're still kind," Jemma said, sliding her eyes between Lottie and Thea uneasily. "They've helped me many times in the past, especially Aunt Imogen." She turned to Thea. "If you come with us, I'll introduce you."

"I still think generally it's not wise to get involved," Thea said, frowning. "After all, somebody's dead."

"It's true. Veronica was a sweet thing," Lottie said, "but really not very intelligent."

"Lottie, no..." Jemma said as her eyes shifted from Lottie to Thea.

Thea held her stylus still on her canvas, staring at Lottie for a moment before continuing.

So, *they didn't like Veronica. I wonder why?*

An uncomfortable silence lapsed between the three women, and Thea began to doubt their burgeoning friendship.

"Do you have plans after class?" Lottie asked. "Jemma and I are going to one of the old dear's afternoon teas. Even if you don't want to investigate with us, I thought you might enjoy meeting some other people on the ship."

"I suppose they're all Askovs?" Thea said warily.

"Some of them," Jemma said. "The majority of them are actually wealthy Originals who can afford the fifth-floor accommodations."

Thea thought for a moment about that. She needed to expand the number of Originals she knew. In a few short months, she would live almost exclusively among Originals, probably for the rest of her life.

"I think that's a good idea," Thea said. "When does it start?"

"Right after this class ends," Lottie said. "But I have to warn you, even though a lot of the fifth-floor passengers are Originals, the old biddies are actually Askovs, except one."

Thea glanced at the other two, wondering what she'd gotten herself into.

An hour later, the three women walked from the painting class to a bank of lifts. They took it to the fifth floor, primarily reserved for Askovs. The main differences between the fifth floor and others were cabins, double the size of those on other levels, a large community center, and a courtyard.

They made their way past a set of cabins with their doors widely separated, leaving the impression of spacious living areas. Thea, who had studied the ship's layout months ago, knew that this floor had much larger suites with two or three bedrooms, whereas her floor contained tiny one-bedroom cabins.

After they strolled past the suites, they entered the courtyard. The courtyard was organized into groups of small tables with two to four chairs. Strategically placed large potted plants gave each table a little privacy. The air smelled fresh, and the lighting perfectly imitated the sun.

"This is lovely," Thea said with a broad grin on her face. "I read about this in the brochure, but it is much better in person."

"Not all of the suites are filled," Jemma said. "You can probably upgrade to something up here."

"Don't really have the credits," Thea said.

Lottie and Jemma exchanged a quizzical look.

"The community center is on the other side of the courtyard," Lottie said. "It has several conference rooms that could be used for parties, school, offices, and group activities. We can take a full tour later."

Thea spotted a gathering of thirty or so people, with some standing and others lounging at tables. Lottie and Jemma ambled to a table with a lone elderly gray-haired woman wearing a dress covered with bright blue flowers. Four or five other women stood or sat at other tables, holding court and directing all of the conversation.

The little snippets of conversation mostly centered around petty fights between families, little skirmishes among family members, disputes among lovers, and loads of other gossip.

Thea breathed a sigh of relief when she saw them. They weren't familiar to her, so there was a very low chance they would know her or her family. She chided herself again for not thinking about the number of Askovs that might be able to recognize her. She just assumed that since the majority of the passengers heading toward Mars would be Originals, she was safe. But she'd been wrong.

"Well, what have we here? I don't think we've met before," the older woman in the blue flowered dress said. "Please have a seat."

Thea, Lottie, and Jemma sat across from the older woman.

"Hello, I am Beatrice Miller," the older woman said, her short, curly white hair arranged like a cloud around her face. Even though she was clearly older, her eyes sparkled like somebody young and energetic.

"Beatrice, this is my friend Thea," Lottie said, gesturing to her. "She's been on Earth for the past few years, and now she's heading to Mars."

"That sounds lovely," Beatrice said. "Please take a cup of tea. We also have these small pink cherry cookies this afternoon."

The three ladies used the meal crafter and selected three cups of hot tea and a plate of cookies.

"So tell me, Thea, what do you plan to do on Mars?" Beatrice asked.

"I'm not stopping on Mars," Thea said, chewing on a cookie. "I'm heading out to Ganymede."

"What do you plan to do all the way out there?" Jemma said, wrinkling her nose. "There's nothing to do except mine."

"That's exactly what I plan to do," Thea said. "I have a job lined up, and they're waiting for me."

"That sounds like a very good job for an Original," Beatrice said with an encouraging smile. "Many Originals manage to save a huge sum of credits and then start a business or use it to start a family. I think it's a smart plan."

Thea smiled, realizing that Beatrice had assumed she was an Original. It was the first time since moving to Earth that had happened, and she would do everything she could to maintain that façade. But both Lottie and Jemma wore quizzical expressions.

"And what about you two?" Beatrice asked. "What are your plans when you get back to Mars?"

"Well, I'm supposed to marry Sam," Lottie said. "This is his last trip as the ship's engineer."

Jemma squeezed Lottie's arm, grinning. "Then the two of us will be real sisters." Lottie chuckled.

Thea remembered meeting the engineer who had arrived with the captain, Samuel Gotham. Thea inwardly laughed at her complete failure to disguise herself on the trip home; she had run across so many Askovs.

"And what about you, Jemma?" Beatrice asked, taking a sip of tea.

"I'm not sure what Mom has in store for me," Jemma said. "She only let me come on this trip because Sam would be here to keep me 'safe,'" she added, making air quotes. "But really, I just wanted to break away from Mars and the limited number of people. I suppose Mom will have somebody lined up for me to marry. It doesn't matter."

"Of course it matters, young lady," Beatrice said. "Marriage is for the rest of your life. You want to make sure you have the right match."

Jemma shrugged, unconvinced.

Thea wanted to encourage Jemma to rebel against her controlling parents, but she was still in the middle of her battle and needed to maintain her secrecy.

"So, can you tell us something about Veronica's family?" Lottie asked.

Thea's shoulders stiffened. She didn't realize Lottie would go into her investigation right away.

"Oh yes, that poor girl," Beatrice said. "She grew up with the best of everything. She was absolutely gorgeous, an excellent sculptor, and, of course, had piles of credits. I don't know why anyone would want to harm her. She was too sweet to have any enemies."

"What about her older brother?" Lottie asked.

"What about him?" Beatrice asked. "Based on everything I've heard, the two siblings got along just fine. Veronica was even fairly close to his wife. I've known the Abbot family my entire life, and I've never heard a bad thing said against any of them."

"They sound a little too good to be true," Thea said, reluctantly joining the conversation.

"Well, you know," Beatrice said with a soft chuckle, "after somebody passes away, they are perfect. I didn't want to add that Veronica wasn't terribly bright, her older brother was a little lazy, and I don't even want to get into their mother, Madison. But still, there's nothing there that'd warrant murdering Veronica."

"Yes, it is very sad," Jemma said in what sounded like false sadness. "Do you know if the family had any debt or business problems?"

"No, as a matter of fact, the family business is expanding," Beatrice said. "They increased their number of credits by thirty or forty percent from last year. It's all so perplexing. The girls and I have been discussing this for several hours now, and we can't figure out what could possibly be the motive."

"Maybe it was just some awful accident," Thea said unconvincingly.

"It could be," Beatrice said. "We really don't know how this ship was constructed. Maybe there was some failure, and that caused poor Veronica to fall down the lift shaft."

Because Thea had spent several months studying the ship's layout, she really didn't think that was possible. But at the same time, she didn't feel comfortable volunteering that information to somebody she had just met.

"I'm sorry I can't help your investigation too much, Lottie," Beatrice said, gulping the last of her tea and placing the cup on the table. "I'm not sure who on the ship could help you."

"It's okay," Lottie said. "It's just the first day. We'll see if I discover anything as the days go by."

"Thea and I will help, too," Jemma said with a sly grin.

"Count me out," Thea said. "I don't want to be involved with something so morbid."

CHAPTER 6

S everal days later, Thea stood in line with Lottie and Jemma, waiting for their turn to enter the Zero-G Maze. The three of them had spent time with each other, enjoying many of the ship's amenities.

"In case some of you don't know, the goal of the maze is to find a hidden object before the opposing team and without getting lost," the Zero-G AI said in a peppy male voice.

Thea exchanged eager looks with Lottie and Jemma. She nervously adjusted her pink and purple spacesuit, making sure she had enough room in the shoulders. From experience, she knew she might need to squeeze through small openings to find their object. It wasn't a real spacesuit; instead, it was just something intended to provide minimal protection from anything she might bump into.

"You have the prettiest spacesuit of all of us," Jemma said with a touch of envy in her voice. "I'm not a fan of this orange."

"Yours is quite beautiful, too," Thea said, gazing at Jemma's spacesuit. "It's not just any orange, but the orange and red that you see during a sunset."

"I agree," Lottie said, also examining Jemma's spacesuit. She patted her blue spacesuit, which mimicked the blue and green of an ocean. "I think all of us got lucky with our spacesuits; we look fashionable."

All three women chuckled.

"Teams one and two," the AI merrily called out. "Please step forward." Lottie, Thea, and Jemma stepped to the front of the line and were joined by three twenty-something men and a young woman.

The seven of them walked through the door, and as it slid open, they stepped into the Zero-G Maze's lobby. It was a dark room with dim lighting. Piles of objects littered the edges of the walls. However, opposite the entrance door, Thea spotted another door-sized opening that seemed to lead to another room.

"Have you read the instructions?" the AI asked.

They all nodded.

"Grasp a wall railing," the AI said enthusiastically as the entry door slid closed.

Jemma and Lottie chuckled, turning to face Thea.

"I can't wait to get started," Thea said with glee. "I haven't played this game in years." She scanned the dark walls.

"The object you're looking for is a golden orb," the AI continued in an upbeat voice. An image appeared on a floating screen in the middle of the room. "The orb will look like this. Keep in mind that it will blend in with many other objects in the room. The first group to find this object wins. Happy hunting."

As soon as the lighting increased in the room, Team Two immediately floated toward the second door opening. Some by holding the railing and others by launching themselves off the walls. They headed to the door leading to the next room, not bothering to examine their current room.

Thea felt a lightness starting from the middle of her chest. She had heard of some people vomiting with the sudden lack of gravity. Deliberately skipping breakfast, she hoped that wouldn't be her fate. But a moment later, a strange sensation spread to her stomach, and something began rising up her throat.

"Oh no," Thea said.

"What's the matter?" Lottie asked, turning to Thea.

At that moment, Thea's nausea eased, and she took a steadying breath.

"Are you alright?" Jemma asked.

"I'm okay now," Thea said. "I felt ill for a minute."

"Should we come back later?" Lottie asked.

"No, no. I'm fine," Thea said. "Let's get going. We're already behind them."

"What was that about?" Jemma asked, pointing to the empty doorway.

"I suppose they think there's a low probability that the object is in the first room, and they don't want to waste time," Thea said, still gazing at the objects now floating around the room.

"Well, that's not a bad strategy," Lottie said. "Maybe we should follow them."

"Makes sense to me," Jemma said, launching herself off the nearest wall.

Unfortunately, Jemma's aim wasn't very good as she shot past the door and collided with the opposite wall.

Thump!

"Are you okay?" Lottie asked.

Thea and Lottie held back a giggle as they gently made their way toward Jemma.

"Moving in zero-G is not so easy," Jemma said. "But I think I'll get the hang of this. Let me try one more time?"

This time, she simply let go of the wall and flapped her arms like a bird trying to scoot the air around her. However, she stayed close to the wall, barely moving.

"That won't work," Lottie said, laughing. "You need to *gently* push off something."

"Oh no," Thea said again as a rumbling feeling made its way up her throat. She tried to hold it in, but a few seconds later, her morning coffee came spewing out of her mouth.

"Hit the emergency button!" Lottie yelled as she made her way back to Thea.

A moment later, Thea heard the alarm, and the gravity slowly returned to one-G.

Thea had hoped she'd feel better with the gravity, but she actually felt worse and crumbled to her knees.

"Thea, what's wrong?" Lottie said, reaching her side.

"Please step aside," Dr. Hadley said, dressed in a blue uniform with her hair in a braid down her back. She stepped through the sliding door with a floating medipad. Pressing a few buttons, she unfolded the medipad into a bed while a number of medical probes extended to Thea.

"Help me get her on the medipad," Dr. Hadley said.

Thea had her eyes squeezed shut as a wave of pain raced around her abdomen. Two sets of hands got her to her feet and helped her onto the medical bed. She felt a probe gently attach to her stomach as the pain subsided.

"Ms. Black, do you remember me?" Dr. Hadley said in a calm voice. "This is very important. What did you eat this morning?"

"Nothing," Thea said in a whisper as her stomach made an agonizing twist. She squeezed her eyes shut again.

"Ms. Black, you've been poisoned with butelacid," Dr. Hadley said. "It's slow-acting, so we should be able to neutralize it, but in the meantime, you might feel—"

Suddenly, Thea rolled to her side and heaved. When her sides convulsed repeatedly, she struggled to catch her breath. But as she reached the dry heaves, the pain began to lessen.

"Are you okay, Thea?" Lottie asked in a shaky voice. "I can contact Mara or Noah if that would help."

Thea's eyes popped open, and she slowly rolled onto her back. She wanted to yell, not to contact her siblings, but she still felt as if she might retch again.

"How are you feeling?" Dr. Hadley asked gently. "You expelled the poison faster than I expected. We must have caught it early."

"That means she was recently poisoned," Agent Walker said.

Thea jerked her head in his direction. "What are you doing here?" Her voice barely above a whisper.

"You nearly died," Dr. Hadley said in a gentle tone. "It's standard procedure to call the IPS."

"Can you answer a few questions?" Walker asked.

"I'd prefer to have her rest a few hours," Dr. Hadley said. "I'll take her down to the infirmary."

"No," Thea whispered before the world went dark.

By early evening, Thea stirred in bed and gradually opened her eyes. She scanned the room, noting the pale green walls adorned with Earth landscape images. Thea took in a multicolored desert that looked as if an artist had brushed paint over the sand dunes.

"Where am I?" she asked in a croaky voice.

"Ah, you're awake," Dr. Hadley said, stepping to Thea from the other side of the room. "You're in the Stargazer's infirmary. How do you feel?"

"Tired," Thea said. "My throat hurts."

"Yes, that sounds about right," Dr. Hadley said. "I didn't finish the repairs to your esophagus. It's better done when you're awake. How's your stomach?"

"Uhmm..." Thea said, rubbing her stomach. "Fine. Like nothing happened."

"Good," the doctor said. "Roll onto your back, and I'll let the medipad complete its repairs."

Thea stared up at the ceiling while the medipad's scanner detected and corrected the burns and tiny tears in her throat.

A moment later, the doctor helped her into a sitting position and handed her a glass of water. Thea noticed three more beds like hers, but she was the only patient.

Staring at the glass, Thea tensed.

"It should be painless," Hadley said. "I need to know everything's working properly."

Thea took a tentative sip, and cool water coated her parched throat. She nodded and downed the rest of the glass.

"Better?" Dr. Hadley asked with a small smile.

Thea nodded. "Did you say I was poisoned?"

"I'm afraid so," the doctor said. "Butelacid is slow-acting but difficult to reverse. The IPS found you drank it with your coffee about ten or fifteen minutes earlier."

"I grabbed a cup on my way to meet Lottie and Jemma," Thea said with a shudder.

"I think the fact that you didn't have a full breakfast saved you," Dr. Hadley said. "Otherwise, there would've been too much poison for the medipad to help."

"Also, being in zero-g triggered motion sickness, causing you to start vomiting before the poison could do its work."

"I just can't believe someone would want to murder me," Thea said with a shudder, and the doctor squeezed her hand. "When can I go back to my cabin?"

"Well…There've been a few changes," the doctor said. "The IPS searched your cabin and found the poison in all of the food and drinks. It would need to be professionally removed, and the Stargazer doesn't have those facilities."

"What am I supposed to do?" Thea asked.

"The IPS will contact you as soon as I tell them you're awake," Hadley said. "They're moving you to the fifth floor."

"No," Thea said, shaking her head. "Can't I move to a lower deck?"

"Oh, I'm sorry," the doctor said. "Your friend Lottie made all the arrangements."

Thea sighed and then chuckled.

"Are you alright?" Dr. Hadley asked, leaning a little closer.

"Yes, I suppose this is really my fault," Thea said.

"You're trying to hide the fact that you're Askov," the doctor said. "Lottie told us while you were unconscious. You were born Dorathea Romly. Why did you change your name?"

"I'm just not ready to talk about it," Thea said, looking away.

"That's alright," Dr. Hadley said. "When you're ready to talk, you can reach me anytime."

"I suppose there's no point in fighting it anymore," Thea said with a forced smile, trying to change the topic. "I'll need to pack."

"Actually, no," Hadley said but paused as if trying to choose her words. "The IPS had to go through all of your belongings. Once they cleared them, Lottie arranged to move them to your new cabin."

"Lottie seems to have taken care of everything." Thea pursed her lips.

"She's been worried about you," the doctor said.

"Charlotte Dover to see Ms. Black," the infirmary's AI said.

"Let her in," Hadley said and turned to the door.

Lottie entered with her wavy black hair hanging past her shoulders. It made her look taller and more elegant.

"Oh, Thea, I'm so happy to see you sitting up," Lottie said, enveloping her in a hug. "I was so worried."

Thea wondered how they'd become friends so fast, but she also felt better with Lottie nearby.

"Has the doctor explained everything?" Lottie asked.

"Yeah," Thea said, rubbing her eyes. "But I can't believe someone tried to kill me. Why?"

"It's strange," Lottie said with wrinkled eyebrows. "First, they involve you in Veronica's murder, then they try to kill you? It doesn't make sense."

"I know one thing," Thea said in a steady, lower-pitched voice. "I'm not going to wait for the next attack. It's time to start my own investigation."

"Happy to hear it," Lottie said with a broad smile. "We can't let them get away with this. I'll help you."

"Now, just a minute," Dr. Hadley said. "Chasing a killer is dangerous. I can't stop you, but considering someone tried to kill you, let the IPS do their job."

Thea and Lottie exchanged looks.

"I can't sit idly by and wait for the murderer to attack again," Thea said with a determined look. "What I don't understand is why someone would want to kill me and Veronica. We'd never even met."

CHAPTER 7

After a good night's rest, Thea sat in bed and gazed around her new room. It was a standard ship's cabin with light gray walls and a dark gray carpeted floor. But now, she resided on the Askov floor, so she slept in a bedroom separated from the living area. Even though she'd intended to travel incognito, she enjoyed this simple luxury. A smile crept across her face as she paced to her separate bathroom.

Several minutes later, she exited her new cabin and into a short hallway. Turning right, she followed the curve of the hall and walked out into the courtyard's sunlight. A broad smile covered her face despite knowing the sunlight was artificial. The shrubs and small trees dotting the courtyard gave the illusion that she was outside. She took a deep breath, and even the air smelled fresher.

"Beatrice," Thea said, walking a little faster. "I wasn't expecting to see you here. It's a little bit late."

"Come over here," Beatrice said, her wrinkled arm waving her closer. "My friends all went to a sculpting class. I just didn't feel like it, but I'd like some company. Have you eaten?"

"No, not yet," Thea said, shaking her head. "But I'm not too hungry, anyway."

"Well, I can recommend the Martian scrambled eggs," Beatrice said. "I've never had anything so good. The Martian soil adds a unique taste that's similar to sausage, even though it has no meat."

"Oh, really?" Thea said with a raised eyebrow as she started scrolling through the menu of the meal crafter. After a second, she found the scrambled eggs and coffee and made her selection, causing them to materialize on the table.

"Smells amazing," Beatrice said. "But I've already eaten. I think I'll just have a cup of tea." She turned to the crafter, scrolled through the menu, and a moment later, a warm cup of tea materialized on her side of the table.

"Mmm..." Thea said with her eyes closed. "This is good—it doesn't taste like this on Earth.

I wonder what they put in here. I'll have to look up the recipe."

"Are you an engineer?" Beatrice asked, laughing. "Always needing to figure out how things work?"

"I had to take some engineering classes at Heliton Academy," Thea said, turning slightly pink.

"Oh, yes," Beatrice said. "Lottie already told us all about you, Dorathea Romly. Why did you change your name? Were you trying to hide from your family?"

"I wish she would've kept her mouth shut." Thea huffed. "But I suppose, in the end, it's my fault for assuming I could travel incognito on a cruise ship all the way back to Anteros."

"That assumption was okay," Beatrice said, tilting her head slightly. "But unfortunately, you ran into two Askovs who recognized you. I think over an eight-month trip, something like that was bound to happen."

"Yeah, you're right," Thea said, hoping not to answer her name change question. "I somehow assumed I'd hide out in my cabin or sneak off to the pool, but the trip is eight months long, and at some point, I would've run into somebody."

"Thea! Beatrice!" Lottie called from the other side of the courtyard.

Lottie and Jemma approached and joined them at the table while Thea finished the last of her eggs.

"I'm so happy that you recovered," Jemma said with a small smile.

"Thank you," Thea said as a warm feeling settled in her chest. It was nice to have someone who genuinely cared about you. "I've never felt that bad before. I hope it's the last time."

"Well, I'm happy you've recovered, too." Lottie grinned. "Because now we can begin our investigation."

"How's that going?" Beatrice asked, leaning forward.

Thea remembered she was part of a troupe of older women who made it their mission to get into everybody's business.

"I know this is just a lark to you," Jemma said with a frown. "But after the attempt on Thea, I think this is a little dangerous."

"I'm afraid I have to agree with Jemma," Beatrice said. "It's one thing to sit around here in our courtyard and talk about an investigation, but to actually actively go after a murderer is just foolishness."

"Well, I don't intend to do anything dangerous," Thea said. "But if I happen to stumble on something after talking to some people, then I'll just let the IPS know."

"Oh, she's just being overprotective," Lottie said. "Don't mind her." She turned to Thea. "I think I know the very first thing we should do—talk to my fiancé."

"What does your fiancé have to do with any of this?" Thea asked.

"He's the head of the ship's engineering," Lottie said as if talking to a five-year-old. "Didn't I tell you?"

"No, actually, you didn't," Thea said. "But to be fair, I didn't ask. The only thing you said is that he's Jemma's brother."

"Well, that isn't important anyway," Lottie said, leaning in a little. "The thing is, if anybody knows anything about the lifts, it's him. Maybe he could give us a little tutorial about how the lifts work and exactly how somebody could've gotten into the shafts."

"Actually, that is a good idea," Jemma said. "Could I join you? I've never actually seen my brother at work."

"You'll have to wait for one of his days off," Beatrice said.

"It just so happens he's off today," she beamed. "Right now, he's just lounging in front of a screen watching some useless show. I already tried to get him to show me around, but he refused. I think if the three of us went to speak to him, we could get him to teach us or, better yet, give us a tour."

"Well, I'm staying here," Beatrice said. "I have a few serials to catch up on." The entertainment serials consisted of episodic shows that ranged from soap operas to educational.

"Sounds like an ambush," Thea arched her brow. "Are you sure he won't get mad?"

"Never," Jemma said, chuckling. "She knows how to get him to do things."

"Well, it's a good idea," Thea shrugged. "If you think he'll be receptive, when should we talk?"

"How about right now?" Lottie asked. "Have you finished your breakfast?"

Thea nodded, and the three women stood.

"You three keep me in the loop," Beatrice said, picking up her teacup. "I want to know what's going on, too."

"Of course, we'd never think of making a move without including you," Lottie laughed.

Thea shook her head with a mixture of excitement at starting a fun adventure and feeling a little uneasy.

———— ✎ ————

Thea followed Lottie and Jemma as they strolled across the courtyard and down another short walkway. Several minutes later, the three stood in front of a door that immediately slid open.

"Honey, I'm home," Lottie called, ambling into her cabin. "I've brought Jemma and a new friend with me."

Thea and Jemma followed as they strolled into an average-looking ship's cabin decorated in shades of gray. It was a little larger than Thea's, and the decor included two small sofas and one overstuffed chair.

Thea heard a shuffle of something like clothing from another room. A moment later, Samuel Gotham, the ship's commander she'd met about a week ago, paced into the room.

"Hello, dear," Sam said, giving Lottie a peck on the cheek. "You're back sooner than I thought."

Sam and Jemma exchanged smiles before he turned to Thea.

"This is Thea," Lottie said with a bright smile. "Remember, I told you about her?"

"Yes, of course," Sam said, nodding his head. "We know each other, but it's been more than ten years."

"Good morning," Thea said, noticing Jemma and Sam's unusual green eyes; they were clearly siblings. "I didn't know you remembered me."

"It was a chaotic evening dealing with Veronica Dover's death," he said with a sigh. "I'm sorry I didn't properly greet you."

"It's alright," Thea said, glancing at Lottie. "I hope we're not interrupting your day off."

"I don't know if you're disturbing me yet," Sam said, turning to Lottie with a half-smile. "But I think I won't have the relaxing day I'd planned."

"Now, don't worry, honey," Lottie said in a sing-song voice. "We won't disrupt your day, we promise. Did you enjoy your show?"

"You want something," he said, chuckling. "Come on, out with it."

"Of course not," she simpered. "I was just asking."

"So you *do* want something," Sam said as the corners of his mouth twitched.

"We just need a little bit of information," Lottie said, blinking up at him.

Sam relaxed into an infectious laugh, gesturing to the sofas set at right angles from each other.

"Let's have a seat," Sam said. "I think I'm gonna need some coffee for this."

After the four of them settled in the living room, Sam swallowed some coffee while Lottie began.

"We were wondering if you could explain how the lifts work," Lottie said.

"What you're asking is a specialized two-year engineering course," Sam said, taking another sip of coffee.

"I think what we really need to know is how somebody could access the lift's shafts," Thea said. "Hopefully, that isn't too complicated."

"But it is," Sam said. "You see, you absolutely must have a bot with you in order to access those lifts. The gravity gradient in those lifts varies significantly, depending on whether one is in use or not, or if the neighboring lifts are in motion. We're generally not able to access those shafts. Instead, we use bots that have special attachments to brace themselves from the changing gravity. What you may not realize is that once you have a bank of independent lifts, each car has to be shielded from its neighbor, and the entire set of shafts has to be shielded from the ship." He downed the last of his coffee and turned directly to Thea. "I know you're trying to figure out how Veronica Dover's body ended up in the shaft. Quite frankly, we're stumped. There's just no way a human body should've been able to enter that shaft."

Lottie exhaled, leaning into the sofa, pouting.

"I don't mean to contradict you," Thea said hesitantly. "I don't have a full engineering degree, but I have taken several engineering classes. Most engineering devices need some sort of emergency access. Are you saying those lifts don't have any?"

"Of course they do," Sam said with mild irritation. "The only way to access the lift is during an actual emergency. The lift's AI would've sent a signal to the captain, Operations, and to the entire engineering team. It would've gone everywhere, and no such message was sent. We checked the log to see if maybe there was a malfunction—there wasn't. We checked the lift itself to see if maybe somehow it had been disabled—no again. Everything is operating perfectly, and somehow, a body ended up inside the lift, which we can't explain."

Though he seemed a little defensive, he had a point; she reflected on his words.

"Well, I don't know," Jemma said. "If the engineers are scratching their heads, how are we supposed to figure this out?"

Sam laughed, gazing at the three women. He leaned forward and selected something from the crafter's menu. A moment later, a warm blueberry muffin materialized in front of him, along with a new cup of coffee.

I don't care who he is; I don't like him, she thought as something inside her hardened.

"Mmm..." He bit into his muffin. "I love it when the berries come out hot and gooey."

"Now you don't have to be rude about it," Lottie said, crossing her arms.

"Honey, think about it," Sam said with a condescending smirk. "You three somehow think you know better than all of the ship's engineering crew and the IPS."

"We'll figure something out," Jemma said.

"I don't know how they do it, but they taste freshly baked." He picked up his muffin and took a second bite. Washing down his bite of muffin with the last of his coffee, he turned to Lottie.

"I'm sorry, dear. I didn't mean to laugh at you," Sam said. "And you're right; it was rude. I apologize to the three of you."

Sam's apology didn't appear sincere to Thea, but she didn't feel it was her place to say anything.

"So, what was your plan?" Sam asked.

"Well, before we talked to other suspects," Lottie said. "We thought we'd get a better understanding of how the lifts work and then maybe open a hatch somewhere and look inside. But now it seems opening a hatch will be completely impossible unless we have a bot."

"Hey, that's an idea," Thea said. "Maybe it was a bot."

"But somebody would still need to control it," Jemma said.

"And there would be a record of that," Sam said, taking another bite of his blueberry muffin.

"Hmm..." Lottie said. "Looks like we're stuck. We'll have to think of a way around this."

"What about the poison in Thea's pantry?" Jemma asked. "How did it get there?"

"How do you access the pantry in each person's room?" Thea asked.

"That's also accessed by a bot," Sam said. "But it doesn't have to be. Each pantry also allows passengers to add ingredients or remove them if needed. But it's a bit complicated. It'd still be significantly easier just to instruct a bot to make the changes."

"So the only thing in common between Veronica and I is that a bot could have committed both murders or attempted murder in my case," Thea frowned.

"Not really," Sam said. "You were both alone and away from your birth families. In other words, these are aspects that would make you both vulnerable. I suggest you three make a list and figure out which common attribute is important."

"You know," Jemma said. "That's something that could help the IPS. Lottie and I knew Veronica better than they ever could, and of course, you know yourself."

"Well, a list could help us get more focus on the investigation," Thea said. "We might also need to look into Veronica's background. I mean, really, why would somebody want to murder her—she seemed harmless. Also, the people who might like to harm me are on Anteros." She chortled.

"Why would somebody want to harm you?" Lottie asked with wrinkled eyebrows.

"Oh, it's nothing," Thea said, shifting uneasily in her seat. "I'm just kidding."

"You know you can always talk to us," Lottie said.

"I know that, and thank you for caring," Thea said, adjusting her collar. "In any case, I'm even more motivated to find out what happened to Veronica and what almost happened to me."

CHAPTER 8

In the afternoon, Thea sat a few meters from the Astro Ball court on the Games and Entertainment deck surrounded by Jemma and the old ladies from the Askov floor. The Astro court was three by twenty meters and covered by dark blue turf. Low railings surrounded the court, preventing balls from rolling away while allowing players easy access.

"Mmm...I love this tangy flavor," Thea said after choosing a strawberry-mango drink from the meal crafter on a small round table.

On the other side of the table, Jemma and Beatrice, with her cloud of white hair, bent their heads together, chatting quietly.

"Is that strawberry?" Lottie asked as she breezed past Thea. "I haven't tried that one yet."

Alice, an older woman in her seventies, sat on Beatrice's other side but maintained a sour expression as she eyed Lottie.

"Where've you been?" Alice asked, folding her arms with glaring brown eyes and pinched lips.. "We don't have all day, you know."

"I'm sorry I kept you waiting," Lottie frowned. "I promise it couldn't be helped."

"Hmm..." Alice said, pursing her lips.

Lottie turned to the remaining ladies with a forced smile. "I'm sorry to keep you all waiting. Do you all know each other?"

"I introduced Alice and Thea," Jemma said. "But I didn't finish."

"Well, I'm Dessie," said the older woman with a thin, bony frame and bronze skin. "This is Fiona." She pointed to the woman next to her.

"Good afternoon, my dear," Fiona said. She was a plump, elderly woman with shoulder-length, curly gray hair.

"I know Imogen isn't here yet," Lottie said, "but I think we should get started."

"Sorry I'm late," another woman with shoulder-length brown hair and striking green eyes speed-walked to the empty chair near Fiona.

Thea turned from the new woman to Jemma, who exchanged a look with her.

"That's Aunt Imogen," Jemma said in a loud whisper. "She's really a distant cousin, but my brother and I call her aunt."

"First, I'm so glad we could meet for a friendly game of Astro Ball," Lottie said with a sly smile. "Second, I hope you're all up for some sleuthing. We need to figure out what happened to poor Veronica."

Thea couldn't explain it, but for some reason, she felt mild disgust. It was as if Lottie had turned Veronica's death into some sort of performance. *Maybe I'm overreacting*, she thought.

"Who should go first?" Dessie asked.

"We will," Alice said, jumping to her feet. "We'll be the red team." She turned to Thea, Jemma, and Beatrice with a brief nod.

Alice stepped onto the blue turf and glanced at two sets of balls. She chose a red ball painted with stars. A moment later, a small white ball, the dwarf star, appeared on the turf. The game's AI placed it randomly, but some positions were more advantageous than others. Alice kneaded the ball between her palms as she squinted at the court.

"Oh, hurry up," Dessie said with mild irritation. "Why do you have to take every game so seriously?"

"Quiet, Desdemona," Alice said. "I'm strategizing."

Dessie sighed and ordered a green frosty drink from a table's crafter.

"Those two go at it every time." Beatrice chuckled.

Fiona and Imogen each selected frosty drinks and settled in, waiting for their turn.

Alice finally threw her ball, and the AI announced it was five centimeters from the dwarf star.

"Ha! I knew it," Alice said, pumping one fist. "Nobody can get closer than that."

Thea hid her smile, watching a frail-looking older woman energetically pump her fist.

Imogen stood, paced to the court, and selected a yellow ball. After a moment, she threw the ball, which overshot the white ball by more than a meter.

"So, how can we help you?" Fiona asked, turning to Lottie.

"We need information about Veronica," Lottie said. "Then we'll compare it to Thea's and see if the similarities give us a clue about the killer."

"But wouldn't you know more about Veronica?" Dessie asked.

"I know some things, but I still need help with her family," Lottie said, squinting her eyes. "For example, my brother, Owen, probably knows, but won't tell me why her family disowned her."

"Oh, that's easy," Imogen said, stepping off the court and regaining her seat. "Before she met Owen, she fell in love with a poor boy. He was an Original from some little town nobody had ever heard of. It was love at first sight for both of them and after sneaking off to meet each other for months, Veronica's parents eventually caught her."

"Do you mind if I go next?" Beatrice asked, turning to Thea and Jemma.

They nodded their consent, and Beatrice walked to the court. She selected a red ball and took her time surveying the court before turning to Imogen, who smirked.

"I know you're up to something," Beatrice said to Imogen with a small smile. She threw her ball, which landed seven centimeters from the dwarf star.

"In any case, Veronica's parents demanded that she give up her relationship with the boy," Imogen continued. "She refused, claiming she was in love. They disowned her, telling her that as soon as she dumped the boy, she was welcome back in the family. Unexpectedly, Veronica ran off with the boy and disappeared from Askov society for about four years."

"Four years?" Thea said, raising her eyebrows. "But she was fifteen years old!"

"The next time she surfaced, she was married to your brother, Owen," Imogen said, turning to Lottie.

"Owen has always been cagey about how he met Veronica," Lottie said. She walked onto the court after Beatrice and selected a yellow ball. She scanned the court for barely a second before throwing her ball. It landed next to the first yellow ball thrown by Imogen.

"Why didn't she get in contact with her family again?" Jemma asked. "They would have taken her in when she married an Askov."

"I might know the answer to this one," Lottie said, stepping off the blue turf and taking her seat. "When Owen and Veronica started dating, she mentioned something about how hurt she was that her family threw her away, and she simply couldn't forgive them."

"Who is her birth family?" Thea asked.

"The Abbots," Imogen said. "They have one powerful Askovian in their family—a Mover, if I'm not mistaken. But Veronica was also a Mover, although a very weak one."

"We have our abilities in common," Thea said, climbing to her feet and pacing onto the turf. "We're—or were—both Movers."

"You're a Mover?" Lottie asked, with a frozen expression. "I thought you were a normal Askov like the rest of us."

"Are we really normal?" Thea asked, laughing as she selected a red ball. She tried to cover her little lie about being an Askov. "Plenty of Originals would disagree with you."

It took Thea a second to see what the yellow team was up to, but she wasn't skilled enough to hit the white ball. Instead, she threw her ball, causing it to collide with Alice's. Thea's ball rolled eight centimeters away, while Alice's remained in place.

"You're lucky you didn't disturb my ball," Alice said with a frown.

Thea wondered what Alice would've done to her.

"You're taking this game too seriously," Dessie said, rolling her eyes.

Lottie absently chewed on a fingernail.

Thea studied her for a moment, confused.

Is she upset because of the yellow team's strategy? Does my Mover ability bother her?

A heaviness settled on Thea's shoulders as she realized Lottie must be upset about the lie. She wished now she'd been honest, but she originally planned to travel covertly.

"So, what do we know based on what we've gathered about Veronica?" Lottie said, visibly collecting herself. "We know that Veronica and Thea are—or were—Askovian, estranged from their families, and alone when attacked."

Thea glared at Lottie for a moment. She'd already explained that she didn't really want to go into her family's background.

Is she trying to get back at me for lying?

Fiona stood and ambled onto the court. She selected a yellow ball and turned to wink at Imogen, who chuckled as if they shared a private joke.

"My dear," Beatrice said, turning to Thea. "I know you don't want to discuss what happened with your family," she said in a gentle voice. "But having us learn more about you might actually save your life."

Thea stared down at the table, wondering if it mattered now since they knew the truth. Or thought they did, thanks to Lottie.

"Very well," Thea said with a sigh. "I think you all know that I used to be Dorathea Romly. My family and I had a huge disagreement. It had a lot to do with what I studied at Heliton Academy. A few weeks before graduation, they disowned me. So, I changed my name and started my new life." She concentrated on keeping her voice steady as she hadn't told them the entire truth.

Fiona threw her ball, which landed with such force that the white ball shot off toward the yellow balls. When it came to rest, all four yellow balls were now within five centimeters of the white one. The red team's balls were all a meter or more away.

"Did Veronica go to Heliton?" Fiona asked, a broad smile covering her face as she almost skipped back to her team, where they high-fived each other.

"Yes, she went there in her early years," Lottie said, trying to hide her smile because it looked as if the yellow team might win. "I think from maybe age five until age fifteen. Then they had that big fight, and she ran away."

"I didn't realize she was so young," Thea said, smiling, distracted by the old ladies' antics. "Do you happen to know who the boy was?"

"No, and Owen's not talking," Lottie said, not looking at Thea.

"Well, he's still grieving," Imogen said with a sympathetic expression.

Jemma strolled onto the court and selected the last red ball. She squinted and tossed. It landed near the yellow balls but about nine centimeters away.

"We won!" Fiona cried, picking up her drink for a team toast.

Alice scowled with her arms crossed, but Thea, Jemma, and Beatrice stood to congratulate the yellow team and join in their toast.

They discussed the yellow team's maneuver and whether they could have disrupted it. But as Thea had suspected, it required more skill than she possessed.

"You know, it's as if the two of you have been living the same life," Fiona said, turning to Thea. "Only you two were about ten years apart."

"What happened to the Abbot family?" Thea asked.

"That one I can answer," Beatrice said. "Veronica's dad and brother are still alive and living in Lunar City. Her mom, Madison, is the matriarch of the family, and she lives in Tymal. She can be quite prickly, but I've only met her a few times. We're related, actually." A half-smile on her lips. "We're third or fourth cousins."

"Her mom sounds like mine," Thea chuckled softly. "It's strange that we have so many coincidences. Now I wish I'd met Veronica. We'd have something to commiserate about."

"Well, physically, the two of you had nothing in common," Jemma said. "You have red hair; Veronica was blonde. You're average height, and Veronica was tall and gorgeous."

"You don't need to rub that in," Thea said with a quirky smile.

"Really, I don't see the point of this conversation," Alice said. "We've gathered a bunch of data points and have no way of organizing them by importance or anything."

"I think this is where I'll have to tell you my secret," Lottie said, clearing her throat. "Let's gather our chairs in a circle."

The red team pulled their chairs closer to the yellow.

"Owen told me something the IPS was investigating," Lottie said. "Veronica's mother, Madison, passed away, and she was set to inherit everything. But the problem is that now Veronica has passed away, the inheritance can't be passed on."

"What? When did Madison die?" Thea asked, turning to Beatrice, who shrugged.

"Some time ago," Lottie said without looking at her. Instead, she turned to Dessie. "What do you think?"

Thea pursed her lips, torn between irritation with Lottie dismissing her and guilt that she lied.

"When did Madison change her will?" Dessie asked.

"As soon as she showed up with Owen," Imogen said. "But by then, Veronica wasn't talking to her mom."

"But wouldn't the estate pass to a cousin or something?" Fiona asked.

"Yes, my mistake," Lottie said, correcting herself. "It can't be passed to Veronica and then to Owen. They grilled him about it for hours, trying to understand if he knew he couldn't inherit if Madison passed after Veronica. Their investigation was inconclusive."

"Is there any sort of funny inheritance in your family as well?" Beatrice asked.

"No, nothing like that," Thea said with a chortle. "The family farm will go to my older brother and sister equally. They're twins."

"That's the reason you left!" Lottie's eyes flashed with a hint of triumph. "Financially, it doesn't matter if you stay or leave the family. You get nothing either way."

Thea froze—not because Lottie was right, *which she wasn't*—but because she assumed they were all finished prying into her past. An uneasy feeling settled in her chest as the other women turned to her with encouraging smiles. She hated this type of attention and definitely didn't want their pity.

"All we've established with this is that two families mistreated their daughters." Thea sighed. "But why would somebody want to kill either one of us?"

"Maybe you're related somehow," Jemma said.

"Probably. Distantly," Thea said. "Most Askovs are related."

"Well, Sam and I were looking into that," Lottie said. "I made a family tree."

Lottie tapped a button on her comm, causing a floating screen to appear beside her. At the center was something that looked like a fallen tree branch with loads of square boxes filled with names and lines connecting them.

"Here is Thea's tree," Lottie said, pointing to the screen. The box with Thea's name turned pink.

"I see the Romly family is also connected to my family," Beatrice said, squinting at the screen.

"Now here is the Abbot family," Lottie said, pointing to another branch of the tree. Veronica's name was highlighted. "Thea was definitely related to her, but they were *very* distant cousins."

"Unless I'm missing something," Thea said. "There's no way I could inherit anything from Veronica's mom or the other way around. I don't think we're looking at this correctly. Let's take a break and get some lunch."

CHAPTER 9

Thea stepped out of a conference room after taking an astronomy class and emerged into the Stargazer's lobby. Walking under the lobby's chandeliers, she smoothed out her black skirt, which had wrinkled after sitting for so long. A moment later, she paced through the Shopping floor's pathway and took the stairs to the Restaurant mezzanine.

She had planned to meet Lottie and Jemma at the Blue Lizard Restaurant the previous day, and she wondered if Lottie was still upset with her. A moment later, she stepped inside.

"We're here," Jemma said, waving to Thea, who then strolled toward them. A moment later, she joined them with a broad smile.

"So, how are you two today?" Thea asked.

"Good," Jemma said with a stiff smile. She eyed Lottie.

"Uh, alright," Lottie said with a slight frown but then forced a smile. "Have you been here before?"

"No, I haven't," Thea said, shaking her head and glancing at the Moonrock decorations. Between each table were artistic boulders strategically placed for a little privacy. The ceiling looked like the darkness of space, but soft gray carpeting covered the floor. "What do you recommend here?"

"I always order the special," Jemma said, grinning. "It's the absolute best."

A moment later, all three ladies selected their food from the meal crafter. Jemma and Lottie also ordered a strange, bubbly purple drink. Thea ordered a glass of water and black coffee.

A moment later, their meals materialized on the table. All three had ordered the special, which included sprouts designed in a lab somewhere on one of the many farms on Mars. This sprout was soft and delicate, with a mild sweetness to it. When paired with a beefy mushroom, it felt like eating meat and vegetables, except it was all vegetarian.

"This is scrumptious," Thea said, chewing on the delicate sprouts.

Jemma and Lottie nodded quietly. Thea gazed at her two friends, who seemed uneasy, and wondered if she should ask them about it.

"So, what did you do this morning?" Jemma asked.

"I got up early to catch my astronomy class," Thea said. "I love that class, but I'm still a little tired."

"Now that you don't have to take classes, why are you taking an astronomy class?" Lottie asked.

"I don't know," Thea said, chuckling. "It's just something I've always wanted to do. Star gazing is a little hobby of mine."

The table fell silent again, and Thea wondered what was going on.

"So, what did you two do this morning?" Thea asked.

Both ladies exchanged looks before looking down at their plates.

"Did something happen?" Thea asked. "Maybe something I should know about?"

"We had an impromptu get-together this morning," Jemma sighed and then turned to Thea. "We've been wondering about your abilities. You're a Mover, right?"

"Yes," Thea said, wondering where this conversation was leading. "Does that bother you?"

"Not all Askovs are comfortable with Askovians," Lottie said, frowning. "Sometimes, especially as kids, the ones with abilities basically torture the sibling without. What was it like for you when you were growing up?"

"For me?" Thea asked, her eyebrows raised. "Well, let me see...My older brother and sister, Mara and Noah, loved to torment me. In case you're wondering, they're both Movers and loved to gang up on me. Worse than that, my mother, who was also a Mover, rarely intervened. So, I had to learn at a very early age how to defend myself. So, I'm very sympathetic to Askovs who have no abilities and were bullied by their siblings. I experienced a version of it, except I made them back off."

"You see, she understands," Jemma said, turning to Lottie. "I vaguely remember when Mara and Noah visited, they mentioned sometimes they had to 'teach her a lesson.' Everyone knew what that meant. But we all just laughed it off."

"How do you know she really understands?" Lottie asked, with a pinched mouth. "She could defend herself, but the rest of us couldn't."

"You just heard me say that my mother never stopped them," Thea said, crossing her arms. "There were two of them against me. I've definitely experienced bullying. What I don't understand is why you think I'd do anything to harm you. What's motivating all of this?"

"Both of us grew up with Askovian relatives," Jemma said with a sad smile. "We were the poor relatives who relied on them for quarterly payouts. While our parents had discussions and negotiations on how much to disperse, the kids played together. That meant we were basically unprotected while our cousins tortured us. In my family, we're all Readers. They could decipher our thoughts, and we had no way of blocking them. Also, many times they'd simply lie to cover up what they did to us. It was quite humiliating."

"I'm very sorry to hear about that," Thea said with a frown. "It's so similar to my experience. I don't know why parents don't take protection more seriously."

"We think that the reason you haven't bullied us is because we generally agree," Lottie said with a scowl. "The question is, what will happen the moment you disagree with us?"

"I've already disagreed with you," Thea said, chortling. "I asked you not to tell anybody about my family, and the next thing I know, Beatrice and all of her friends are discussing them. Nothing has happened to you."

Lottie looked down at the table and turned pink.

"You see?" Jemma said. "She's not trying to harm us. I think you and Sam are overreacting."

"Well, Owen agreed with us," Lottie said. "And he should know because he was married to Veronica, who was a Mover."

"He didn't exactly agree," Jemma said.

"Did Veronica ever harm Owen?" Thea asked with a worried expression.

"No," Jemma said, her hands fidgeting. "He was very clear that Veronica was nothing but sweet to him."

"Yes, but she was a weak Mover," Lottie said, leaning forward. "Maybe she never harmed him because she really couldn't."

"I just want to understand something," Thea said as a tightness settled on her chest. "The two of you, plus Sam and Owen, got together this morning to discuss whether or not I am dangerous?" She couldn't keep the hurt out of her voice and stared at the two of them in disbelief.

"No, no," Jemma said. "It wasn't like that at all. We just got together for breakfast, and then somebody brought up the fact that you were a Mover. The conversation just went in that direction. I'd still like to remain friends."

"I had no idea you were taking this seriously enough to actually reconsider our friendship," Thea murmured.

Another silence fell over the table, and Thea looked down at her plate as an emptiness settled on her.

"Well, I don't want to end things on a bad note," Lottie said, avoiding Thea's eyes. "But Jemma and I have spa appointments."

"Of course," Thea said, nodding. They all put their plates in the recycling and stood.

Lottie and Jemma left the restaurant first, while Thea ambled in a different direction.

What could've happened to make them change so much? she thought.

As soon as Thea stepped off the lift onto the Askov floor, Beatrice approached her at a fast pace.

"Oh, my dear, I'm so happy I ran into you," Beatrice said, grinning. She grasped one of Thea's hands and dragged her to the courtyard.

When Thea arrived, she immediately spotted the five ladies who normally ruled the courtyard.

"Look who I found, everybody!" Beatrice said as they stepped toward a series of tables pushed together.

Thea sat next to Beatrice, and Fiona was on her other side.

"How are you, my dear?" Fiona asked, swallowing a little pink, syrupy drink while her gray curls bounced on her shoulders.

"Okay," Thea said in a flat, monotone voice. "Did something happen?"

Imogen giggled, not noticing Thea's mood.

Dessie's bronze skin wrinkled with a smirk as she gazed at Thea. "We know who murdered Veronica and very likely tried to murder you."

Fiona and Imogen nodded their agreement with Dessie. But Beatrice shrugged her shoulders.

"I think you're all crazy," Alice said, her brown eyes squinted with her scowl. "There's no way you can be right."

"Who do you think it was?" Thea asked.

"Captain Ebert, obviously," Fiona said. "Think about it. Who has access to the lift? Who can control a robot and then erase the fact that the robot was controlled? And, more importantly, who can access the private pantry in your room?"

"What?" Thea asked. "I don't believe it."

"Good! Someone else with some common sense," Alice said and smacked the table. "A man of that standing would never lower himself to murder. He's more likely to use his influence to get what he wants."

"Well, I don't know about a man of his standing," Thea said. "But my objection is that there's no motive at all. I don't even know if Captain Ebert is an Askov, and I highly doubt we're related."

"Well, you'd be wrong, my dear," Beatrice said with a small smile.

"It turns out you and Captain Ebert are second cousins," Imogen said.

"What?" Thea said, confusion marring her face. "Is he an Askov?"

"Yes, my dear," Dessie said. "We looked it up. He's related to you on your father's side of the family. What's not clear is what he'd gain by harming you."

"So the reason we have you here is if you could tell us more clearly exactly why you changed your name," Beatrice asked in a gentle, coaxing voice. "If you tell us more about you, we might be able to save you from a killer."

For the first time, Thea actually mulled over her words seriously. Yesterday, when Beatrice had made that request, Thea simply assumed she was being nosy. She still didn't quite trust the ladies, but they might be able to help her.

"I just don't know," Thea said. "The idea that it could be Captain Ebert is mind-boggling. And even if you know what happened between me and my family, I don't see how you could help me if he really is the killer. You don't have any proof, and the IPS is not going to just walk onto the ship's Bridge and arrest him."

"And that's the other thing I warned them about," Alice said with a scowl. "Without any proof, all they'd be doing is either insulting Captain Ebert or alerting an actual killer. This line of thinking is dangerous."

"And we have a remedy for that," Fiona said in a bubbly voice. "We could break into his quarters and search for clues."

"Break into—" Thea said with raised eyebrows. "There's no way I'm going to be a part of that. More importantly, what type of clues do you think you're going to find? Taking control of a robot, the lift, or even the pantry doesn't leave suspicious smudges or fingerprints. It's all done electronically. The only clues he'd leave behind would be a digital footprint, which nobody at this table is equipped to detect."

The ladies' eyes met for a moment.

"Look, I think we're missing something important," Imogen pursed her lips. "The reason that you look for clues is because you don't know what's there. I still think it's valid to look for clues."

"And if you get caught breaking into his quarters?" Thea asked.

"Well, that's all just part of the fun of it," Fiona said and chuckled.

"You're crazy," Alice said, placing both hands on the table and pushing to her feet. She turned and stalked off to her cabin.

"I've known the captain for years," Beatrice said with a slight frown. "He can be a little eccentric, but I can't imagine him as a killer. Breaking into the captain's cabin is a bit much, but it doesn't change the fact that we need to look for clues."

"I might know somebody who can dig around for a digital footprint," Imogen said. "A friend of a friend."

"I think I might know somebody who's actually a crew member," Dessie said, scrunching her eyebrows.

"Oh, those are both good resources," Fiona said. "I think both of you should ask them and see what we can do about finding a digital footprint."

"Wait a minute," Thea said, raising her hands. "When I mentioned digital footprint, it wasn't so that you can go and break the law."

"Don't worry, Thea," Imogen said with a twinkle in her eye. "I've got an idea that includes you."

"What? What do you have in mind?" Thea said with mild trepidation.

All four ladies chuckled and rose to their feet, and drifted away from the table.

"Don't worry," Beatrice said as she trailed after her friends. "I'll keep an eye on them."

"The corporation that owns the Stargazer protects digital signatures," Thea said, raising her voice to their retreating backs. "This is a bad idea." She added in a quiet voice.

CHAPTER 10

Thea sat in the courtyard of the Askov floor by herself. It was shortly after lunch; the older ladies who normally spent time there had gone to various classes. She knew she'd have a couple of hours alone, so she began to watch a show. It was one of her favorites, an adventure about a teen boy who traveled interdimensionally. However, she couldn't get lost in the story. Instead, she kept replaying the last conversation she had with Lottie and Jemma. She still couldn't believe that they thought she was dangerous.

"What did you do?" Lottie shouted as she stomped toward Thea.

Thea jumped, turning toward her.

"You heard me! Why did you tell the IPS about Owen?" Lottie yelled again.

"Wait. We don't know that she did that," Jemma said, holding up one hand.

"Of course we do," Lottie said. "The IPS showed us all the evidence. It's definitely her."

Thea stood, blinking with confusion at the two women.

"Do you have anything to say for yourself?" Lottie glared at her, crossing her arms.

"What exactly are you talking about?" Thea asked, eyebrows wrinkled.

"What are we talking about?" Lottie said with a cold, hard stare. "You know exactly what we're talking about."

"It seems the IPS called Owen in for questioning," Jemma said matter-of-factly. "They have evidence that you provided, showing Owen with the chief of Communications in her cabin."

"What?" Thea asked. "I still don't know what you're talking about."

"Then I'll break it down for you," Lottie spat. "The IPS called Owen in for questioning again because someone sent them new evidence showing he was having an affair with Petra Kroft, the head of Communications. I used to work in Comm, and I clearly recognized your digital signature from all the messages you and I have exchanged."

"My digital signature?" Thea asked. "How is that even possible? I haven't communicated with the IPS in days now."

"Don't play dumb," Lottie said in a harsh tone. "Nobody's going to believe that innocent act you're trying right now."

"I think Thea's behavior proves she's innocent," Jemma said. "She didn't harm your brother. Before coming on this ship, she'd never met Owen or Veronica. And remember, she has no way of benefiting from this murder."

"They already had evidence suggesting he could inherit from Veronica," Lottie said with a pinched face. "This latest evidence is going to get him locked up."

"This is the second time my comm signature's been duplicated," Thea said, as a frisson of fear raced down her spine. "It happened when Veronica died and now with Owen. This feels like a deliberate attempt to frame me again."

Lottie scoffed.

"I think she has a point," Jemma said, turning to Lottie. "This is the second time. It's as if somebody is out to get her."

"Nobody's out to get her," Lottie said, leaning a little closer to Thea. "Instead, somebody's out to get Owen. My brother has never done anything to you. Why are you attacking him?"

"Attacking him?" Thea said, feeling anger bubbling in her stomach. "I'm not doing anything to him. I was literally sitting here minding my own business when you stormed up to me."

"What I want to know is, what are you going to do about it?" Lottie said, her eyes boring into Thea's.

"Well, since you told me about everything half a second ago, I don't have any plans," Thea said, crossing her arms and returning Lottie's glare.

"Go to the IPS and tell them you made up the whole thing!" Lottie said, staring daggers at Thea.

"I can't do that," Thea said with an edge to her voice. "I'm just going to tell them the truth."

Lottie raised her hand as if she was going to slap Thea across the face. Thea raised both hands with her palms facing Lottie. A second later, Lottie lifted off the floor, her legs becoming level with the rest of her body. Lottie began flailing about, screaming.

Thea shielded her mind as she felt somebody trying to poke into her thoughts.

"Stop screaming!" Thea yelled, finally losing her temper.

"Don't tell me what to do!" Lottie screamed back. "Put me down!"

"Thea, please put her down," Jemma said, wringing her arms.

"Stop shouting," Thea said, continuing to elevate Lottie in the air while she flailed.

After a few minutes, Lottie finally stopped shrieking and quit thrashing her arms around as much.

"You see? Askovians are dangerous," Lottie spat out.

A moment of guilt washed over Thea, but at the same time, she was too scared to just let Lottie go.

"You attacked me first," Thea said in a raised voice. "I was just defending myself."

"Well, I can't do anything to you now," Lottie said. "Put me down."

"Are you going to try to hit me again?" Thea asked.

Lottie shrieked—no words, just a banshee screech.

"Lottie!" Jemma raised her voice and got Lottie's attention. "It's not fair to blame Thea based on the IPS's evidence. Why don't you calm down? Promise not to hit Thea and ask her nicely to let you go."

"I won't hit you! Now let me go!" Lottie said, glaring at Thea.

Thea still didn't quite trust her and peered at Jemma.

"I think that's as polite as she's going to get," Jemma said.

Since she didn't want to keep using mental energy to suspend Lottie in midair, Thea slowly lowered her arms with her palms, continuing to face Lottie. As her feet touched the floor, Lottie ended up standing two meters away.

"You will pay for this," Lottie said, venom dripping in her voice. She turned on her heel and stalked out of the courtyard.

"I need to call Agent Walker," Jemma said, glancing at Lottie's receding back.

"Why?" Thea asked, running a hand through her hair. "I wish I understood what was going on."

"Technically, we weren't supposed to tell you about Owen," Jemma said. "But Lottie was so angry she confronted you anyway."

Pressing a button on her bracelet, a floating screen appeared immediately in front of her. The image of Agent Walker filled the screen.

"I'm afraid Lottie and I told Thea about Owen," Jemma said in a hesitant voice.

"I asked you not to bring this up with Ms. Black," Agent Walker said with a pinched face. "You've ruined hours of investigation time with this little stunt." He sighed, looking defeated.

Jemma gazed at Thea, guilt all over her face.

"Very well," Agent Walker said. "Since you two have started the conversation, Ms. Black, let's meet in...two hours."

Thea nodded and the floating screen went dark.

"I'm sure you're innocent," Jemma said. "Meeting Agent Walker will only clear the air."

"I can't believe our friendship has come to this," Thea said, exhaling a large breath.

"I think once we clear the air, we can all go back to being friends," Jemma said with a sympathetic smile. "Lottie's very close to her brother, and she can be a bit emotional if she thinks he's being harmed."

"It feels like everything has changed between us," Thea huffed. "For more than a week, I thought we were becoming friends. We did things together and enjoyed each other's company. Actually, Lottie helped me move from my first cabin to the new one. I don't understand why it's all so different now."

"Unfortunately, she had a really bad childhood with Askovian cousins," Jemma said in a quiet voice. "It didn't go well for her brother, either. And given that you're Askovian, they're ready to believe the worst of you, even with the flimsiest of evidence. I'm very sorry about that."

"It's not up to you to apologize," Thea said as her shoulders drooped. "I guess I'd hoped this would all blow over and we could go back to being friends. But it doesn't seem as if that's going to happen."

Jemma studied the floor for a minute. She studied the back of Thea's floating screen that was still hovering over the table where Thea had been sitting.

"So, what were you watching?" Jemma said, trying to change the conversation.

"Oh, that's just a show about Johnie, who has adventures as an interdimensional traveler," Thea said. "Since communication between the Stargazer and Earth is intermittent, I only got the latest episode today. It's about a week old."

"Yes, I think that's how the IPS found the evidence against Owen," Jemma said. "I really wish we had just followed Agent Walker's advice and waited for him to talk to you. Now I don't know what's going to happen."

Thea nodded as a heaviness settled on her chest. She was grateful to have at least one friend left but still couldn't believe how quickly Lottie had turned against her.

A couple of hours later, Thea walked into a conference room on the IPS floor. Agent Walker and Clark sat next to each other, quietly chatting. Walker stood when Thea entered, and Agent Clark nodded.

"Please have a seat," Agent Walker said, gesturing to a chair on the other side of the table from the two agents.

"Would you like something to eat or drink?" Agent Clark asked, gesturing to the meal crafter.

Thea shook her head while lowering onto her chair.

"I understand from Charlotte Dover and Jemma Gotham you've heard about our ongoing investigation into Owen Dover," Walker said.

Thea nodded but didn't volunteer any more information.

"I just want to be clear," Walker said. "You're not in any trouble. It's becoming increasingly clear to both of us that someone is trying to frame you. However, we can't ignore this evidence. The message about Madison Abbot's will and Owen's affair arrived with your digital signature. But the message was sent from Earth, and you're obviously here."

"Also, it shouldn't be possible to duplicate these comm signatures," Clark said. "They're one of a kind. Which is why we couldn't ignore this."

"I know what you mean," Thea said. "It doesn't help that I recently changed my digital signature because I changed my legal name. I don't know if something went wrong in that process, but I've double-checked my comm signature a few times, and everything appears correct."

"Yes, we checked your comm as well," Walker said. "It's just not clear to me what is going on."

"Also, if somebody is trying to implicate you, they're doing a terrible job of it," Clark said. "They've put you at the scene of a crime where there is evidence that shows you weren't present. Now they've duplicated your digital signature, but that, coupled with the first crime, makes us doubt it even more."

"That is another thing that surprises me," Thea said. "The so-called evidence is very inconsistent. I'm happy to hear that you two have noticed the irregularities, but I just don't understand why Lottie and sometimes Jemma don't seem to notice."

"Well, Ms. Dover seems overly emotional at the moment," Agent Clark said, glancing at Walker.

"I found Jemma Gotham to be reasonable, though," Agent Walker said. "Have you been having a problem with her?"

"No, not really. It's been mostly Lottie," Thea said and paused for a moment. "Okay, if you don't believe this is really my digital signature, why did you call me here?"

"We still needed to check your statement," Walker said. "This way, when our supervisor reviews our work, there won't be any questions."

"Would you please allow me to examine your comm?" Clark asked.

Thea snapped her blue-tinted bracelet open and handed it to Agent Clark. The agent placed it over the table, which emitted a faint whitish light that enveloped Thea's bracelet.

"What is that?" Thea asked.

"It's a scanner," Walker said. "It's checking the digital signature on your comm. But it's also going to check for anything else, like spyware, viruses, and anything else that really shouldn't be part of that bracelet."

A moment later, a chime sounded throughout the room.

"It looks like it's done, and there are no issues," Clark said, furrowing her eyebrows. "But there was something a little funny."

"What do you mean?" Thea asked.

"It seems when you had your bracelet changed, instead of getting a brand-new one, you just had your existing one overwritten," Agent Clark said. "That could create some unfortunate open doors in the software that controls this comm."

"I know. I was worried about that," Thea said. "However, I took it to a second dealer and had them check for that specifically. You see, a...friend gave me this comm. That's why it has a teal tint, whereas everybody else's is clear. I had hoped to maintain the same security level. But maybe I opened myself up to something like a virus."

"No, it's clear of everything," Clark said. "There are no viruses. It's just something to keep in mind."

"We understand there was a brief altercation between you and Ms. Dover," Walker said.

"Yes, she tried to slap me," Thea said, staring down at the table. "I just can't believe how far things have come. In any case, I was trained at Heliton to defend myself. So I did the first thing that crossed my mind. I suspended her in midair and blocked my mind. I don't know if there are any Readers on that floor, but I felt someone trying to mentally poke me."

"We're just letting you know that Ms. Dover has filed a complaint against you," Agent Walker said.

"A complaint!" Thea said as the anger boiled in her stomach again.

"Don't worry. We reviewed the footage," Agent Clark said. "It was definitely self-defense, but I would advise you to stay away from her as much as possible."

Thea nodded, setting her mouth in a grim line.

CHAPTER 11

The following afternoon, Thea met Jemma in the Askov courtyard. They sat at one of the smaller round tables with a meal crafter in the middle.

"The coffee's really good here," Thea said as the warm liquid radiated through her chest. She'd worn a pale pink, comfortable dress to cheer herself up.

"Mmm...this is just what I needed," Jemma said, swallowing her first bite of warm apple crisp with vanilla ice cream. She had dressed casually in a T-shirt and shorts, with her brunette hair pulled back in a ponytail.

"What did you want to talk about?" Thea asked, drinking some coffee. She wasn't in the mood for small talk. "I already figured out last night that you're a Reader, and you tried to intrude into my mind."

"Well," Jemma said hesitantly, "I want to apologize. When Lottie tried to attack, you subdued her by raising her off the ground. I got scared for Lottie only because I've been hearing from her and my brother about how awful Askovians are. So I tried to influence your mind, but you easily blocked me. I'm sorry for entering your mind without permission. That was rude and intrusive, and it could've been dangerous. I am sorry for that."

Thea raised an eyebrow at her words. When she was in school, Readers who intruded into others' minds usually felt it was their right. They saw it as self-defense to know everyone's thoughts. When Thea felt that intrusion, she immediately shielded her mind as a result of her training in school.

"That is what confuses me," Thea said, examining Jemma. "You're Askovian. You're a Reader."

"Yes, sort of..." Jemma said with a lopsided smile. "I am in between two worlds. Technically, I am Askovian. I can detect other people's thoughts. But the reality is I'm weak. It's easy to block any of my intrusions. I have to concentrate very hard just to get any impressions from the other person, and it's very difficult for me to block anybody trying to intrude on my mind.

The result is that Askovians don't respect me, and Askovs with no abilities are slightly afraid of me."

"Why are you and Lottie friends?" Thea asked.

"Our families have known each other since our parents were kids," Jemma said. "All of us grew up together, which is why it wasn't surprising when Lottie and Sam started dating and eventually got engaged."

"Is your brother also a Reader?" Thea asked.

"No, Sam is an Askov like Lottie," Jemma said, taking a bite of her apple crisp.

"So you're Askovian, but you get a pass," Thea said with a smirk. "I am Askovian, but I'm dangerous. That's how Sam and Lottie see me."

Jemma looked down at the table as her face turned pink, and then she nodded.

"What about Lottie's brother, Owen?" Thea asked, rubbing the back of her neck. "Is he Askovian?"

"No, not at all," Jemma said. "Although his wife Veronica was. But she was a weak Mover, so she was accepted into our circle."

"I can't believe our little friendship has come to this," Thea said, frowning. "But I can accept it. There's no point in spending time with people who are afraid of me."

"I'm very sorry about that," Jemma said.

"Please don't apologize for them," Thea said. "They're allowed to feel what they feel. But they're not allowed to hurt me."

Jemma nodded, taking another bite of her apple crisp.

"On a different note," Thea said, "have you thought about the investigation into Veronica's murder?"

"No, I got caught up with Owen's trouble. Have you come up with anything?"

"Yes, I've been thinking about the contradictory or even random evidence. I wonder if there's something more important that we're missing. The way Veronica was murdered, and even the attempt on my life, feels like a distraction from something important."

"Really?" Jemma said, furrowing her eyebrows. "What do you think the killer doesn't want us to see?"

"I don't know," Thea said, slowly scratching her head. "It depends on the motive. If the motive was credits, then the most obvious suspect should've been Owen. But Owen had an alibi, Petra Kroft. And he seemed really upset by his wife's death. For some reason, I just don't think he did it."

"Also, I don't think he knew he couldn't inherit from Veronica."

"What if the motive was love or hate or something like that? Do you think there's any chance it could be Kroft?"

"I didn't really know her, and like you said, Owen seemed genuinely upset."

Thea nodded with a small smile.

"There's always the motive of power, of course," Jemma said. "But all of us are from lesser Askovian branches. We're distantly related to the Spencers, who are extremely wealthy, but we aren't. The Dovers are related to the Pendletons, who are also wealthy, but Lottie and Owen aren't."

"True," Thea sighed. "Neither one of them could've passed on any sort of power to anybody else. It's very perplexing."

"Maybe we're looking at this the wrong way. Maybe Veronica was never the intended victim. She was in the wrong place at the wrong time."

"But she was murdered when she was alone in her own cabin. I don't see how a murderer could make that mistake."

"Well, I meant maybe they intended to go after Owen. But he went to Kroft's cabin."

"Well, what about Captain Ebert?" Thea asked. "Is he wealthy, or does he command a certain amount of political power?"

"I don't think he's wealthy," Jemma said, "But he has a little political power. He's related to another Askov family. I think they're Viewers."

"Isn't Kroft Chief Communications?" Thea asked. "I was thinking in terms of how the murder was done. Somebody with very high-level access could have orchestrated the crime. Although I have no idea why Ebert or Kroft would want to harm Veronica."

The two women sat in silence, lost in thought, as Thea sipped on her coffee while Jemma finished the last of her apple crisp.

Later that evening, Thea stepped into a large conference room with bland gray walls, dark gray carpeting, and no windows. She glanced at four long rows of tables and selected a seat in the front row.

She sat between a young girl who may have been twelve and an older man, clearly of retirement age.

Alice stood at the front of the class next to a gigantic floating screen. Normally a somewhat surly woman, her intelligent brown eyes shone in class as she transformed into a bubbly and engaging teacher when discussing her favorite topic—astronomy.

Thea peered down at the tabletop, checking to make sure her electronic telescope was connected to one of the ship's scanners.

The Stargazer commanded multiple scanners with a three-hundred-sixty-degree spherical field of view. The astronomy class allowed students access to one scanner, depending on availability. The ship's AI analyzed the information from the scanners, but the astronomy class taught students to analyze the data manually. They learned to detect sunspots, evaluate passing asteroids, and survey supernovas millions of light-years away.

"Is everybody here?" Alice asked, a broad smile on her face. "Does everybody have their telescope ready?"

Thea's mind always had to adjust between the sour woman she encountered in the courtyard and this sunny, cheerful woman who was completely in love with her subject.

"Today we're going to be looking at the aftermath of a supernova in the N-three-two sector," Alice said. "Using what we learned last week about manipulating our telescopes, I want you to find the star alpha-four-eight-three. Call me if you need help."

Alice began walking along the tables while the students started their electronic telescopes.

Thea and her classmates almost vibrated with excitement as they looked forward to today's lesson.

Carefully selecting the initial settings for the telescope, Thea triple-checked to make sure she had the right filter for alpha-four-eight-three and then started the viewfinder.

"Mine isn't working!" a little boy at the end of Thea's row called out.

Alice immediately scurried to him and began a quiet conversation.

Thea's telescope also appeared to stall, but she remembered something from the previous lesson. Carefully disengaging the filter, she restarted the telescope's search pattern.

The star appeared immediately, but it lacked enough definition. Instead of relying on the standard filter for supernovas, she slowly measured the star's luminosity and selected the appropriate filter for this particular supernova. A second later, it all came into view.

The view was glorious. She had never seen anything so beautiful as the star's brightly colored rings shimmering around it.

A small grin covered Thea's face, and she wished she had time to capture the colors in a new composition. She settled for taking several images and sending them to her cabin.

"And so, how are things going with you?" Alice asked as she stepped to the other side of Thea's table.

"I think I found it," Thea said with just a hint of pride.

Alice peeked at the images from Thea's telescope and grinned. "It looks like you figured out the trick. Keep up the good work, Thea." Alice nodded and turned to the next person at the table.

Thea chuckled softly as she studied the image from her telescope, feeling lucky to have taken such an enjoyable class.

"Thea. What are you doing here?" Imogen asked as she walked into the courtyard.

Sitting at a small table in the middle of the morning, Thea munched on toast and scrambled eggs. She had stayed up late the previous night in her astronomy class and now reviewed her notes.

"We have something to tell you," Imogen said as Fiona and Jemma followed close behind. They grabbed another table, joining it with Thea's. Once seated, they each ordered tea and buttered cookies from the crafter.

Thea pursed her lips, mildly irritated, as Imogen chatted excitedly while Jemma avoided meeting her eyes. Fiona, with her shoulder-length gray hair and friendly personality, seemed unchanged.

"You'll never guess what we discovered," Fiona said, grinning as her eyes burned with a low intensity. "Captain Ebert was supposed to meet with Veronica the evening she passed away. Can you believe that?"

"Really?" Thea asked. "I didn't even realize those two knew each other."

"Well, I don't think they did," Fiona said with her face scrunched. "They were going to meet at a get-together that included a few other crew members and their spouses. Turns out, the crew members are also Owen's friends."

"But at the last minute, there was a small emergency in engineering. It meant all the crew members were called away, including Captain Ebert."

"Can you tell me something about the emergency?" Thea asked.

"We really don't know," Imogen said with a small smile.

The two older women were clearly enjoying their little piece of gathered evidence.

"How did you find out about this?" Jemma asked, still not meeting Thea's eyes.

Thea assumed Jemma still felt embarrassed about their talk yesterday, but she was too annoyed to talk to her directly.

"One of the crew members is Beatrice's niece," Imogen beamed. "They get together a couple of times a week to talk. Her niece mentioned the canceled get-together. That got Beatrice's attention, and she started asking more questions."

"This gives Owen another link to Veronica's death," Thea said. "I'm sure one or more of those crew members would've had the clearance to activate the entrance to the lifts, access my pantry, or even tamper with a robot. I wonder if the killer caused the emergency, leaving Veronica by herself."

"I know the crew members," Jemma said, meeting Thea's eyes for the first time. "They're mostly juniors."

"And that's what we've been thinking," Fiona said in a conspiratorial tone. "We think Captain Ebert created the fake emergency, met Veronica, and killed her."

"I think you're taking this too far," Imogen said, rolling her eyes. "There's no reason for Captain Ebert to kill her."

"There's no reason we know of," Fiona said, emphasizing the last words.

"Well, at least it's a new direction to start poking around," Thea said thoughtfully. "Maybe we should do some kind of background check on Captain Ebert."

"That's going to be a little difficult because the access to the Net is intermittent," Jemma said.

"True, but there is a Net here on board," Thea said. "We could at least get started. I don't know anything about the captain myself."

CHAPTER 12

"Bridge, please," Thea said, stepping onto the antigrav lift after breakfast. She wore her only formal jumpsuit while hastily smoothing down the navy top, hoping to hide a few wrinkles.

"Please wait a moment while I verify your clearance for the Command Deck," the ship's AI replied in a mechanical voice. The lift's door slid closed, leaving her isolated for a moment. She flashed back to the scene of the body falling through the ceiling and nearly dashed back out again. But a moment later, the lift began to move.

"You have been cleared for Command," the ship's AI said. "Captain Ebert will meet you when you arrive."

Thea took several steadying breaths, surprised by her reaction to being alone in the lift. She'd taken the lift alone since encountering Veronica's body, but something about the stationary lift unsettled her. She shifted from foot-to-foot at the thought of meeting Captain Ebert. How well did he know her family?

The lift's doors slid open, revealing a large curved floating screen that dominated the far wall of the bridge.

"Ms. Thea Black," Captain Ebert said with a broad smile. "It's my pleasure to welcome you to the ship's bridge."

They exchanged nods. She stepped onto the deck, glancing around with wide-eyed amazement. The bridge was shaped like an enormous cube. Throughout the room, she spotted a set of five floating screens, each with a crew member quietly analyzing the data displayed on them. A large elevated chair dominated the center of the room, which included its own floating screen and an armrest full of multiple buttons Thea couldn't even begin to comprehend.

"I'm so glad you got my message," Captain Ebert said. "Beatrice mentioned that you might like this tour, and I thought it'd be an easy way to help compensate for some of the problems you've experienced on our trip. I promise the

Stargazer normally has a quiet and uneventful journey."

This must be Beatrice's way of furthering their investigation, she thought.

"Thank you so much for the personalized tour," Thea said, repressing the little thrill of excitement that raced through her. "You didn't need to invite me on a personal tour, but I'm very grateful."

Captain Ebert chuckled and then gestured toward his chair. He led the way, and Thea followed closely behind.

"I'm sure this is obvious, but this is the captain's chair," Ebert said with a lopsided grin. "From here, I know the status of navigation, engineering, communications, operations, and every single station needed to run this ship. Technically, the AI does all of that, and I'm just the human backup, but don't tell them that." He chuckled at his little joke. Thea joined him with a small smile.

He turned to an officer on his right. "This is Chief Comm Officer Kroft, and as you know, we have very intermittent coverage from Earth right now," Ebert said. "It's because we've been going through a prolonged solar storm. However, we think we'll have a little window in a few hours."

So, this was the woman the IPS accused Owen of having a relationship with, she thought.

Kroft was a tall, willowy woman in a navy blue uniform. She turned briefly to Thea as her short blonde braid shifted over her shoulders. Less than a second later, she turned away without even a nod, giving Thea the impression she wasn't important enough for Kroft.

"What does the communications officer do on a regular basis?" Thea asked, turning to Ebert.

"She monitors the solar storm," Ebert said. "She's using some of those scanners we made available to your astronomy class."

Thea did her best to hide her surprise. It seemed Beatrice and maybe some of her other friends kept Captain Ebert apprised of her activities. It felt like her childhood in Anteros, where everyone knew what she was doing and eagerly reported back to her parents.

"I suppose maneuvering the Stargazer is handled exclusively by the AI?" Thea asked.

"No," Captain Ebert said, gesturing to another officer. "The Chief Navigation Officer, Quincy, acts as a human check to the AI's work." Quincy was a gray-haired man with a genial smile.

"He monitors the AI's output and verifies we're still on course," Ebert said. "Technically, he's not needed," Ebert added in a loud whisper.

Quincy gave him a mock glare with a small smile before turning back to his work.

"This officer does sciency things, I suppose," the captain said with a smirk.

"I'm Ulrick," he said, rising to his feet and nodding to Thea. His formal mannerisms contrasted a little with the captain's relaxed presence. "Chief Science Officer, and for some reason, the captain has no idea what I do." He smirked.

"This is the Chief Operations Officer," the captain said. "Rogers monitors passenger systems and addresses issues as quickly as possible. He's also responsible for all our crew's social events."

Rogers, a large man with a round belly, nodded to Thea before returning to his screen.

"When do you use the screen?" Thea asked, gesturing to the large floating screen that dominated the far wall.

"When everything's going as planned, we mostly use it as a beautiful decoration," Captain Ebert said, chuckling. "But when things aren't going well, we can use it to focus on parts of the ship involved with burgeoning issues. For example, once, years ago, we experienced an unexpected asteroid coming toward us. We used the main screen to capture images of the asteroid detected by our scanners."

"What did you do?" Thea asked, her interest piqued.

"Altered course. It cost the company more fuel, but better safe than sorry."

"What types of shipboard problems have you experienced?"

"Well," the captain said with a raised eyebrow, "the last time we needed to use the main screen, there was a brawl in a bar. I would've never thought a bunch of Askovs would start a fight over who won the last football game. We had to lock some of them up just to get them to calm down. At least it broke up the routine and boredom."

"I wish I'd been around to see that." Thea chortled.

"It was a sight!" Ebert said. "Do you want to continue the tour?"

"Yes, please," Thea said, completely drawn into the tour despite her wariness of Captain Ebert.

The captain introduced the remaining officers on that floor, and then they took the stairs up to a partial floor immediately above the bridge. It didn't have a wall facing the bridge. Instead it had a sturdy, clear railing. When they reached the top step, Thea watched as several crew members rushed back and forth between various floating screens.

"These are the junior members of our crew who are basically learning from the seniors on the floor below," the captain said, spreading his arms to include all of the crew members on the upper level.

Thea remembered that these were the crew members who Lottie would have invited to that get-together with Veronica. And now, she knew another reason Beatrice had arranged this tour.

"We don't have time to discuss each one of their functions," the captain said, waving toward them dismissively. "This floor exactly mimics the floor below, where the senior staff work. And periodically throughout the day, either they come down, or the senior staff come up and engage in a little training or ask them to get some additional work done. But I would like to take you to my office." The captain gestured to the stairs. "There's something urgent I need to discuss with you."

Thea followed Captain Ebert back down the steps to the main bridge floor and through another door not too far from the lift. As they approached it, the door slid open, and she nearly gasped at the sharp difference in the decor. It looked as if she had stepped back in time as she took in the dark faux-wooden paneled walls adorned with old-fashioned paintings, complete with gold gilding on the frames. She paced onto the soft, deep-red carpet on the floor toward a large wooden desk that dominated the room. He took a seat in a large leather chair, and she grabbed a chair opposite.

"Would you like something to drink or eat?" the captain asked.

"Yes, water, please," Thea said.

The captain selected the menu on a meal crafter camouflaged by an old-fashioned ship's compass. It looked like a brass cylinder with a thick footing and a glass dome over the top. A needle spun randomly from left to right, never quite stopping, making it clear it wasn't working. A moment later, a glass of cold water materialized in front of her and a hot cup of coffee in front of Captain Ebert. They each drank while

Thea wondered about this talk and the real reason he'd given her on the tour.

"We've never been introduced before this journey," Ebert sighed as if settling into a story. "I couldn't introduce myself during Ms. Dover's...In any case, I'm your father's cousin. But he always referred to me as Uncle. I've been in contact with your dad off and on for the past several years, ever since you went to Heliton Academy."

"Do you mean you've been keeping track of my whereabouts and reporting back to my dad the whole time I was at Heliton?" Thea asked, as her chest tightened.

"No, not like that," Captain Ebert said quickly. "Six years ago, when you traveled from Mars to Earth, I was the captain of that ship. I just kept an eye on you during the trip to make sure you were safe, which is what your dad wanted."

Thea lowered her shoulders.

"Things are different now." The captain scowled. "Your dad wants me to report to him so that I can pressure you to comply with your family."

"Never!" Thea said as she shot to her feet.

"Hold on! Let me finish!" Ebert said as he climbed to his feet, although not as fast. "Let me tell you everything, and also, let me help you."

Thea eyed the door, debating whether to run from the room or sit down and hear him out. After a moment, she regained her seat but sat on the edge, her shoulders stiff and her back straight.

"Your dad wants me to apply pressure so that you'll do what he wants," the captain said. "I won't do that. Instead, let me ask you, how can I help you?"

Thea examined his face for a moment. She sifted through the accusations from Imogen, Fiona, and Dessie and compared them to his actual words. She decided to trust him. "I'm not sure right now. My plan is to arrive in Anteros, hide with a friend, and take another ship to Ganymede."

"What's waiting for you on Ganymede?" Ebert asked.

"The perfect job," Thea said with a tentative smile. "There's a small mining colony run by Brimble Mining. They want to be more self-sufficient, which includes starting their own farming operations. Obviously, I come from several generations of farmers, and I've studied farm engineering in school. I know I can do a good job."

"I'm sure you can," the captain said with an encouraging smile. "How long will you be in Anteros?"

"Unfortunately, I have to wait two months," Thea said, pursing her lips. "I know that makes me vulnerable, but that ship's schedule was the fastest I could find."

"I don't think that plan will work anymore," the captain said. "Your family will be looking for you. Somebody already told them that you're on this ship and that you have a new name. They know when you'll be arriving."

"I was afraid of that," Thea said as a heavy feeling settled on her shoulders. "I didn't really expect so many Askovs on this ship. And even then, I still didn't think things through. The Askov community is small, so someone was bound to recognize me, and they'd know my family. Originally, I didn't stay on the Askov floor, hoping to avoid them. But then there was the murder, and my plans fell apart."

"Don't worry," the captain said. "I won't tell anybody about our talk today. The less everybody knows, the safer you'll be."

"Thank you. I appreciate that," Thea said, nodding her head.

"Of course," Ebert said. "Now, Beatrice tells me you're acclimating well to the Askov floor. I know you're regretting the move there, but let me point out that you were recognized long before that move. Beatrice and her friends discussed you a day or two after we launched."

"Really?" Thea said with raised eyebrows. "That must've been Lottie. This really was one of my dumbest plans."

"Now, don't be too hard on yourself," the captain said. "It's hard to know how things will fall when you're in a brand new situation."

"Yes, well, now I wish I had just stayed on Earth," Thea said, frowning. "I may have been safer, but..." *Really, I still wouldn't have been safe.*

Chapter 13

Thea sat alone in the Askov courtyard as she sipped her second cup of hot chocolate while munching on toast with cheese and bell peppers. She chewed slowly, letting the mildly sweet yellow bell pepper mingle with the sharp cheddar cheese in her mouth.

Focusing on a small floating screen, she followed the love story between a twenty-something woman and a slightly older man betrothed to someone else. She'd spent months trying to resist following the story because of its predictable plot, but something kept drawing her back to it. Thea had enabled the dampers on her floating screen so that nobody else would be disturbed by her soap opera. However, an urgent vidchat request from Imogen interrupted her show.

"Hello," Thea said, hoping Imogen's interruption would be brief.

"Thea!" Imogen groaned. "Help! I'm stuck in my bathroom."

"What?" Thea asked in a raised voice. "I don't understand. You're stuck in a bathroom?"

"The fire alarm!" Imogen said, gasping for breath. "I can't breathe—help me!"

Thea watched Imogen's reddening face and shot to her feet, dashing to Imogen's quarters. She tried to ignore the sinking feeling in her stomach as she raced across the courtyard and down a short hallway. Glancing at the floating window, which followed her. Imogen coughed as Thea banged on the door, but it wouldn't open.

"How do I get in?" Thea said, thumping the door with her fist. "Can you hear me?"

Imogen nodded, looked down at something, and a moment later, the door to Imogen's cabin slid open. Thea sprinted past the dining room and through the living room to the bathroom door. She began pounding on the door.

"Imogen! Imogen!" Thea yelled.

But when she turned to her floating screen, it was empty. Instead, a strange reddish gas filled the space. In an instant, Thea knew what had happened. Somehow, the fire system had activated, releasing ceridium, a reddish gas that bonded with all oxygen molecules, choking out the fire. However, a human caught in the same gas would die. Raising her hand and frantically banging on the door, Thea finally realized she needed to call for help. She selected a button on her comm.

"Emergency services," Thea yelled.

"What seems to be the problem?" the ship's AI responded.

"The fire alarm is activated on the other side of this door," Thea said, "but there is somebody trapped inside."

"Negative," the ship's AI said. "The fire system has not sent a notification."

"Can you scan the bathroom on the other side of the door?" Thea asked, with shallow breaths. "Hurry!"

A couple of seconds later, Thea finally heard the ship's AI in a loud voice.

"This is a ship-wide announcement. There is an emergency on deck five. Please remain where you are until the emergency is under control."

"What can I do to help?" Thea asked, her eyes wide. "Can you manually activate the door? Should I get the medipad?"

"Negative. The door has malfunctioned," the ship's AI said. "Please wait until the IPS arrives."

Thea called Imogen's name several more times while banging on the door, but she heard nothing, and when she turned back to her floating screen, she still couldn't see her.

Her chest tightened as she started to fear the worst. *I don't understand what could have happened*, she thought.

A moment later, Agent Walker and five other IPS agents raced into the room.

"Stand aside, Ms. Black," Agent Walker said and turned to another IPS agent near him. "Clark?"

"Ms. Black, please step this way," Agent Clark said.

Thea didn't respond and didn't step away from the door. It was as if she were frozen in place, unable to comprehend anything. A gentle hand reached for hers, cutting gently into her frozen thoughts.

"I wonder if you could step this way with me so that the other agents can help Imogen

Stone," Agent Clark said. "You do want to help Imogen, right?"

Thea turned to her and focused on Clark's words. It suddenly dawned on her that she was in the way, and she followed the agent to a chair in the nearby dining room. They both watched as Walker, four other agents, and a silver-colored human-sized robot installed a large screen over the closed bathroom door. The robot had a general human shape but looked like a soldier wearing metal shielding. It extracted lasers from its arms to cut apart the bathroom door in seconds. More of that red gas billowed out of the bathroom, but the screen absorbed all of it and returned the bathroom to normal oxygen levels.

In the middle of their work, Dr. Hadley jogged into the room.

"How are you doing?" Dr. Hadley asked with furrowed eyebrows.

"Okay," Thea said in a shaky voice.

"I expect you're in shock," Dr. Hadley said. "Let me give you something for it in a moment. Right now, I need to check on Ms. Stone."

Thea nodded.

Agent Walker and four other agents removed the screen and gingerly stepped into the bathroom with Dr. Hadley in tow. The robot stowed its lasers inside its arms and made its way to the cabin's open entrance to prevent passengers from entering. Thea couldn't see into the bathroom, but a second later, an IPS agent raced out of the room, selected a floating medipad from the wall, and quickly pushed it back into the bathroom. Thea listened to some of their conversations, but they were disjointed, and she couldn't figure out if Imogen was still alive. Also, she heard voices coming from the cabin's open door. When she turned, she saw a growing crowd of other Askov passengers.

"Aunt! Aunt!" Jemma yelled. "Let me in. Let me talk to her."

She suddenly burst through the crowd, pushed past the robot, took a moment to scan the room, and raced to the bathroom. However, Agent Clark caught her before she interfered with the IPS' investigation.

"You'll need to come with me," Agent Clark said in a firm, steady voice.

"No, it's my aunt," Jemma said. "What's wrong with her?"

Agent Clark firmly wrapped one arm around Jemma's and guided her toward the dining room into a chair next to Thea's.

"But what's happening?" Jemma asked, tears rolling down her cheeks. "Why wasn't I notified? I only came this way because I saw the crowd."

Thea glanced at Agent Clark, wondering if she should say something.

"It appears the fire system malfunctioned in Ms. Stone's bathroom," Agent Clark said gently. "We don't know what her condition is at this time. We're waiting for the doctor to examine her."

"The fire system malfunctioned?" Jemma said, repeating slowly as if she couldn't comprehend. "I've literally never heard of that. That system is used all over Earth, Lunar City, and Anteros, and I've never heard of it malfunctioning before."

"I agree with you," Agent Clark said. "It's extremely unusual. But we've barely started our investigation, and we might discover it was something else."

"Aunt Imogen is the only family member left who still talks to us," Jemma said as her voice quavered. "Nothing can happen to her."

Thea frowned, turning to Jemma. She considered hugging her, but their relationship had been so rocky recently.

"And what are you doing here?" Jemma asked with a hint of accusation in her voice.

"Imogen called me," Thea said quietly. "I ran as fast as I could, but I couldn't access her cabin at first, then I couldn't open the bathroom door. I really hope she's okay."

"She called you?" Jemma said with raised eyebrows. "Why would she call you and not me?"

"I really don't know," Thea said, shaking her head. "None of this is making sense. The fire system has a safety rating that's measured in decades. I also have never heard of it malfunctioning."

Jemma started crying and covered her face. Thea reached to comfort her.

"Don't touch me!" Jemma shouted. "As far as I know, this could all be your fault. Did you try to kill my aunt?"

"What?" Thea asked. "I would never do anything to harm her. Why would you even think that?"

"You're Askovian," Jemma said sternly. "Those of us without abilities know how cruel your kind can be."

Thea blinked several times, shocked at the words coming from Jemma's mouth.

"Jemma!" Lottie said as she squeezed through the crowd, rushed past the robot, and burst into the room. "What's going on? Is Imogen okay?"

Jemma covered her face again and began sobbing. Lottie took the seat next to Jemma and wrapped her arms around her while Jemma continued to weep. After a moment, Lottie noticed Thea sitting on Jemma's other side.

"What are you doing here?" Lottie asked with a sneer. "Only family should be allowed in here."

"Miss Black found Ms. Stone," Agent Clark said. "We have more questions for her, so she's not going anywhere at the moment."

"You found Imogen?" Lottie asked. "You mean you killed her! That's exactly what Sam was talking about. Askovians want to kill the rest of us."

Thea sighed, climbed to her feet, and turned to Clark. "I think it's best if I wait in my quarters. You can question me there."

Even though she didn't have Agent Clark's permission, she turned and left Imogen's cabin.

In her cabin, Thea reclined on a sofa with her feet on the coffee table. She munched on a warm, buttered croissant while she went over the earlier events. What had made the fire system malfunction? Why couldn't she open the doors to the cabin and bathroom? Why had Imogen called her instead of one of her relatives? Why were Jemma and Lottie so quick to blame her? A knock at the door brought her out of her reverie.

"Yes. Come in," Thea said, rising to her feet.

The door slid open, and Agents Walker and Clark entered.

"Is Imogen alright?" Thea asked.

"Sorry, no," Agent Walker said, shaking his head.

Thea blinked back tears and gestured to the two chairs opposite the sofa. She regained her spot on the couch.

"Can we record this interview?" Agent Clark asked.

"Yes." Thea nodded.

"I understand Ms. Dover and Ms. Gotham became agitated at your presence," Agent Walker said. "Would you tell us why?"

Thea sighed and didn't reply for several seconds.

"I'm not simply prying," Walker said. "This may be important to our investigation."

"I know," Thea said in a low voice. "They found out I'm Askovian, and they can't forgive me for it. Also, it didn't help that Imogen called me first. They both asked if I..."

"When we first met, you listed your status as Askov," Walker said.

"I'm sorry," Thea said, staring down at the coffee table. She shook her head, remembering the mistakes she'd made preparing for the trip.

"Why did you try to hide something like that?" Agent Clark asked.

"My plan was to travel without being noticed by any Askovs," Thea said. "Imagine my surprise when I found some of my official information incomplete. I chose to change my status to Askov, hoping it'd be easier to hide."

"You also hid this from Ms. Dover and Ms. Gotham," Walker said as his blue eyes bored into Thea's.

"I only met the two of them at the start of this trip," Thea said with a huff. "It literally never came up. They think the fact that I'm a Mover means I'm going to hurt them. But I've never even threatened them."

"I understand from Commander Gotham that they were harassed as children," Walker said.

"Yes, Jemma mentioned that," Thea said, pursing her lips. "But just because some Askovians are aggressive doesn't mean we're all like that. Some of us were bullied, too." Her mind flashed back to her older brother and sister.

"Would you run through the events of the morning, starting from the time you woke up?" Walker asked.

Thea explained that she had woken later than usual because of her astronomy class. Then she ended with trying to get into Imogen's bathroom.

"Do you know why she contacted me instead of her friends?" Thea asked.

"We have a theory that the killer compromised her comm," Walker said. "We'll know more in a few days."

Thea shook her head slowly. "Is that why her cabin and bathroom doors didn't open?"

"No, the fire system's connected to the doors," Agent Clark said. "It activates the doors to contain the oxygen that may be fueling a fire."

"Do you know what made the system malfunction?" Thea asked.

"We're still looking into it," Agent Walker said.

"Have you noticed how brutal the attacks were on Veronica and Imogen?" Thea asked. "I was in excruciating pain when I was poisoned. Even though all three attacks were different, the killer planned for us to suffer before dying. I just wonder why."

Agents Walker and Clark exchanged looks.

"We discussed that on our way here," Agent Clark said gently. "But we don't have any ideas yet."

"One more thing," Agent Walker said. "Ms. Gotham and Ms. Dover are completing forms to charge you with murder."

"What?" Thea narrowed her eyes.

"Don't worry," Agent Walker said. "There's no evidence that points to your involvement."

"Something about this level of hatred feels off," Thea said, exhaling slowly. "I haven't done anything to them."

CHAPTER 14

The following day, Thea strolled alone around the Observation deck, the highest passenger floor. The oval-shaped room allowed her to retrace her steps five times while going over the events of the previous day as a heaviness settled on her chest. She occasionally peered through the clear dome overhead, examining the star clusters she'd studied during her astronomy class.

"There you are!" Alice called out.

Thea jumped and turned to her friend. She liked this version of Alice, who was friendly and genuinely helpful to students interested in astronomy. She'd attended many classes on the Observation deck with Alice and other students.

"Hey," Thea replied with a faint smile. "I didn't think anybody would be here today."

"I know what you mean," Alice said with a lopsided smile. "I like to hide here to get away from all the girls' chatter. But now that I think about it, sometimes the girls follow me here. We may not have too much time before they show up." She chuckled softly.

"You're such a tight-knit group," Thea said, resuming her amble with Alice. "How did you all meet?"

"When we were children, in Anteros," Alice said. "Beatrice and I had the same tutor. We've known each other since forever. Fiona was really Imogen's friend first." Her voice caught on Imogen's name, and she cleared her throat. "Dessie was actually the younger sister of a friend who passed away. So, we all just naturally blended together." She sighed and stared out at the stars.

Thea felt a pang of sympathy for her and turned toward the stars with her. Her thoughts drifted to the friends she'd left on Earth—she really missed them. Also, despite the terrible words they'd said, she also missed Jemma and Lottie's friendship.

"I'm really going to miss her," Alice said, quickly wiping her eyes. "Sometimes she got on my nerves, but she was kind and helpful. She'd go out of her way to get things for you or make things happen for any of us in need. I can't believe she's gone."

"I know what you mean," Thea said, sighing. "She was alive one minute and then gone the next. What's going on with this ship?"

"I don't know," Alice said, furrowing her brows.

"There've been two deaths and an attempted murder," Thea said. "When I spoke to Captain Ebert, he said this was highly unusual. On such a long trek—eight months—and the average age of the passengers..."

"Steady there, my girl," Alice said with a lop-sided grin. "We're as young as we feel."

"I know," Thea tried to hide a smile. "I just meant you have more experience than the rest of us."

They both giggled.

"Thank you," Alice said. "I feel a little better."

"Sometimes a good laugh breaks the sadness," Thea said.

"What were you saying earlier?" Alice asked.

"Oh, yes," Thea said. "Captain Ebert said that it's not unusual for somebody to pass away on this journey, but usually it's just natural causes."

"I know the murders are highly unusual," Alice said. "But there's something familiar about them. It feels like the reign of terror from the Stone kids. Both types of attacks were vicious."

"Stone—" Thea stopped, interrupted by a loud caller.

"Alice, Thea," Fiona cried as her gray curls bounced with her stride. "We've been looking everywhere for you." Dessie and Beatrice followed.

"There's a rumor that the IPS has found a suspect," Dessie said with a grim expression.

"How in the world did you hear about that so soon?" Alice asked.

"Shouldn't that be confidential?" Thea said, pursing her lips.

"Not when we're around," Beatrice said with a hint of pride in her voice. "We've all got contacts, and we can find out what's happening all over the ship, including within the IPS. We're going to find Imogen's killer first."

"Yes, we're a force to be reckoned with," Fiona said with her hands on her ample hips. All of the old ladies raised their heads with pride, and Thea suppressed a laugh.

"But think about it," Thea said, redirecting them to her earlier point. "If you can find out what's happening within the IPS, so can the murderer. Leaked information will allow the killer to continue getting away with breaking the law and will make the rest of us unsafe."

"Oh, you're exaggerating," Fiona said, shaking her head. "It's not like we go around telling everybody."

Thea raised an eyebrow at that, especially considering they were in the process of telling her.

"Well, we could be a little more discreet," Dessie said, frowning.

The ladies quieted for a moment.

"So this is where you've been hiding out," Beatrice said, glancing out at the stars. "It's beautiful here. I should come here more often."

"Yeah, sometimes I just come here to think," Alice said with a sad smile.

"I miss her too," Fiona said, clearing her throat. "I can't believe she's really gone."

"Well, you know she'll never really be gone from us," Dessie said in a quiet tone. "As long as we remember her, she'll live on in our hearts."

"Right now, that drivel's not working for me," Beatrice said in a hard voice. "I feel angry that somebody took her away from us well before her time. We should do something about this."

"I've been trying to come up with a plan, but right now I'm drawing a blank," Thea said. "Maybe there's something we can do to assist the IPS instead."

"Oh, I don't know," Alice said. "They have access to the latest technology. I don't see how we could help them."

"Alice Tucker," Agent Walker called as he stalked toward them in a brown uniform. "May we have a word alone with you?"

Agent Clark, with her hair in a tight ponytail, followed close behind.

"Is she under arrest?" Fiona asked, stepping in front of their group. "If not, she'd rather they questioned her here with the support of her friends."

Alice turned toward the ladies surrounding her and then turned back to Agent Walker, nodding their heads. The two agents came to a stop a meter away from the group.

"Ms. Tucker, I strongly suggest that you come with us," Clark said. "We need to ask some questions that you may not want known by all of your friends."

"I have nothing to hide from my friends," Alice said, crossing her arms.

"They're just trying to scare you," Beatrice said in a loud whisper. "They could just as easily ask the questions here."

Thea wondered if maybe Beatrice and Fiona were simply trying to gather more gossip. But maybe Alice's friends genuinely wanted to keep her safe.

"Very well," Walker said, drawing his lips into a straight line. "Would you tell us what you did with your time yesterday morning until you found out that Imogen Stone had passed away?"

"Yesterday?" Alice said, scratching her hair. "I had a class last night. Thea was there." She turned to Thea, who nodded. "Then I woke up late, around maybe ten, and made some breakfast for myself before planning my next lesson. I was busy until maybe twelve when Beatrice told me that Imogen had passed away."

"Do you want to add any more information?" Clark asked.

"Add information?" Alice asked. "What is this about?"

"We have evidence from your comm signal," Walker said. "We traced it leaving your cabin, traveling to Imogen's, and tampering with the fire system."

"That's outrageous," Fiona said in a raised voice.

"There's no way Alice would have that kind of access," Thea said.

"Actually, she does," Clark said. "Maybe the Operations Officer mistakenly set her permissions, but she has as much access as the captain."

"Even if I have that level of access, I didn't know about it," Alice said, turning to her friends. "I couldn't use something I didn't know existed."

All of the ladies shook their heads while exchanging looks with each other.

"I think this is all convenient," Beatrice said. "Has Alice had those permissions during the entire journey?"

"Yes, and we have evidence she's used these permissions before," Agent Walker said. "You've been accessing the scanners. Instructors should never have that ability."

"How exactly was I supposed to know that?" Alice said, her voice full of indignation. "Sometimes Rogers was busy, and I needed a last-minute change. He never complained about it."

"That's because he didn't know," Walker said. "In any case, you need to come with us to the IPS floor. We have a lot more to discuss."

"What do you intend to do with her?" Fiona asked, with much less bravado than before. "I'm positive she's innocent. She'd never harm anybody."

"We just want to question her," Agent Clark said. "This won't take long.

"Ms. Tucker, please come with us," Agent Walker said in a commanding tone.

Alice gazed at her friends as fear etched her face. A few minutes later, the two agents and Alice walked toward the lifts. The doors slid open, and they disappeared.

"Oh no, what are we going to do?" Dessie asked. "How can we help her?"

"You don't think she really did it?" Fiona asked haltingly.

"Of course not. She's completely innocent," Beatrice said, with a hint of anger.

"Somebody is trying to frame Alice," Thea said, with wrinkled eyebrows. "We need to find out who this is before somebody else dies."

"I can't believe she's gone," Jemma said with teary eyes.

"There, there," Beatrice said, giving Jemma a gentle hug. "I know this sounds like a platitude, but in time, the sadness shall pass, and you'll only remember the good times you shared with Imogen."

Thea sat in the courtyard at a small table by herself. She was close enough to hear the conversation with Jemma and the rest of the older ladies, but she was thankfully out of their line of sight. She didn't want to endure any more of their accusations.

"Oh, Jemma, I'm so very sorry," Lottie said, holding Jemma's hand. "This has been our worst trip yet. One thing after another keeps going wrong."

"I can't believe they arrested Alice." Dessie set her mouth in a straight line. "Somebody is trying to frame her."

"That's not what I heard," Lottie said, turning to the other ladies. "The IPS has evidence that Alice had a very high clearance and could access a lot of the ship's functions. The crew gave her that access for her class, but she could've also used it to access the fire system, robots, or anything else."

"Where did you hear that?" Jemma asked, raising her eyebrows.

"I have contacts too," Lottie said, looking down her nose at the older ladies.

"Anyway, that's not important right now," Dessie said. "What's important is how do we free Alice from the IPS? They've arrested her; there's no way she did it. Even if she had access to all the things you mentioned, there's no way she even knew she had that kind of access. Alice is a very simple soul—she likes the stars, and that's it. Knowing her, she would've used her permissions only for her class even if she'd access to the entire ship."

"Yes, I think you're right," Beatrice said, turning to the other ladies, who nodded with her.

"And it's our job to help get her free," Fiona said. "Maybe Thea can help us."

"Oh no, not Thea," Lottie said urgently. "I understand the IPS still might arrest her."

Thea gasped, but fortunately, the commotion from the table covered the sound.

"What?" Jemma asked. "Why'd they even be looking in her direction?"

"Because a Mover could've done both murders," Lottie said. "She could've pushed Veronica down the lift shaft and activated the fire system using her abilities. She's not out of the woods yet."

Thea began to feel her blood boil as she heard their conversation.

"Oh, I think your source is mistaken," Beatrice said with a mirthless laugh. "Thea was also a victim, remember?"

"Are you sure she was a victim?" Lottie said in a voice heavy with accusation. "Nobody else saw her take that poison."

Shocked by Lottie's words, Thea considered going to their table and yelling her innocence. Then Thea remembered that she was gathering valuable information that might help her get Alice out of the IPS's clutches.

CHAPTER 15

A couple of days later, Thea stepped into Captain Ebert's office late in the afternoon after his shift ended. She approached with a fast-paced stride, intent on discussing her own investigation into Imogen's death, hoping the captain could provide some information.

"Thea. Please come in," the captain said, rubbing his eyes and slowly lumbering to his feet. "I'm sorry I had to make you wait. It's been a difficult few days after Imogen's death." He gestured to a chair on the other side of his desk.

"What's been difficult?" Thea asked, taking her seat. "The funeral preparations?"

"No, thank goodness," the captain said with a heavy sigh. "We have comm access now, so we alerted her estate attorneys on Anteros, and they're threatening a lawsuit. The company's involved, and it's basically a mess."

"You said attorneys. Was she that wealthy?" Thea asked with knitted brows.

"Yes," Ebert nodded. "She inherited from two wealthy families. First, her husband died in an accident, and she got everything. Next, she inherited property from her parents when they passed away."

"Hers is the only death where beneficiaries have a lot to gain," Thea said with a thoughtful expression.

"Sort of," the captain said, rubbing his forehead. "Her cousins will inherit, but none of them are on this ship."

"What about Jemma?" Thea asked.

"There are something like fifteen cousins in line for her credits before it would ever reach Jemma," Ebert said.

"I see," Thea said, frowning. "Well, I know you must be tired. Do you mind if I start with my questions?"

Captain Ebert nodded.

"Last night, I spent quite a bit of time thinking about Imogen's murder," Thea said. "To me, the murders and the attempt on my life all appear random at first glance. But when I think about it, all of those deaths happened because somebody had high-level access to the ship's systems. Now, I assume the IPS has already considered this. The reason I wanted to talk to you is to ask for a list of crew members who have high-level access to the ship's proprietary functions."

"You're right, the IPS has already considered this," Ebert said, leaning back in his chair and exhaling in a puff of air. "I can't give you the list; it's proprietary, but I did give it to the IPS. I'll tell you the same thing I told them: about half of the crew members have that access. It's the only way we can run a lean ship, and there are a lot of duties that fall to multiple crew members. Their access has to accommodate their shifts, the time of day, and a number of other circumstances. The other half of the crew, without the high-level access, probably has sufficient authorization to cause the murders." Ebert leaned forward with his elbows on his desk, peering directly at Thea. "And I'll tell you what I told the IPS. I personally handpicked all of my crew. I'll vouch for all of them. They'd never do anything to harm another person."

Thea returned his gaze, wondering how he could be so sure of about fifty crew members. "Could you give me some examples of how a crew member would have access to multiple systems?"

"Sure, let's take Kroft, Chief Comm Officer, for example," Ebert said, staring up at the ceiling for a moment. "She's obviously responsible for ensuring that we have clear communications to both Earth and Mars. Besides letting us know when there will be an out and when we'll be clear, she also assists with interdepartmental tasks. She facilitates communications between engineering and navigation. The AI does most of the work, but Kroft makes sure both departments actually have the information they need. As Comm, she also expedites information between operations and control and a host of other activities."

"Do you have records of who has been accessing the ship's high-level functions?" Thea asked.

"Yes, of course, we keep meticulous logs," Ebert said, showing mild irritation. "I've already handed those logs over to the IPS, and there's nothing irregular about them."

"I'm stumped," Thea said, exhaling. "The only people who had access to the ship's high-level functions are your crew, and at the same time, you tell me that the killer couldn't be part of your crew. Do you have any idea who could have sabotaged those systems and caused the deaths of Veronica and Imogen?"

Captain Ebert drummed his fingers on his table, staring off into space with his irritation clearly visible. "I wish I knew," he said in a harsh voice. "I'm so close to retirement, and I just can't end with this on my record. Two murders, both on my watch!" He balled up his fist but didn't continue.

"Could somebody have stolen any sort of access codes from any of your crew members?" Thea asked. "Is one of your crew members dating a hacker? I'm just desperately trying to figure out how somebody could've gotten that level of access."

"So am I," Ebert said, his lips thinned to a straight line. "I've racked my brain for answers, held private meetings with crew members, and analyzed the access logs manually. I simply can't figure out what's going on." He relaxed his palm and turned to her. "Are you worried I'm going to sweep this under the rug?"

"It's not really that," Thea said, surprised by the intensity of his words. "The issue is I don't really have any sort of connection with the IPS, and from my point of view, it looks as if nothing's really happening."

"Oh, trust me, they're investigating," Ebert said with a mirthless laugh. "They've interviewed me and several of my crew members multiple times. They definitely feel that the culprit has to be among us, but I feel that somebody is manipulating one of my crew members."

"Do you have any idea who that could be?" Thea asked.

"No, no idea at all," Ebert said, leaning back in his chair.

Thea and Captain Ebert continued their conversation for just a few minutes before they said their goodbyes, and she stood to leave.

"Okay, I'll let you know if I find something," Thea said. "And I hope you do the same." A heavy weight descended on her shoulders as she realized she hadn't made any real progress on her investigation.

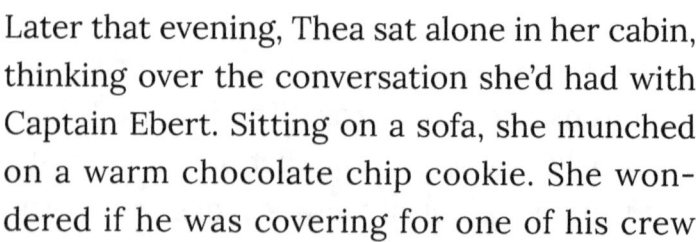

Later that evening, Thea sat alone in her cabin, thinking over the conversation she'd had with Captain Ebert. Sitting on a sofa, she munched on a warm chocolate chip cookie. She wondered if he was covering for one of his crew members or if he genuinely felt that they were all completely innocent. She activated the meal crafter, and a fresh cup of tea appeared on the coffee table. It was interesting that Imogen was the only victim who left behind substantial wealth, which could be a real motive. Of course, that didn't explain Veronica or me.

A knock on the door interrupted her thoughts, causing her to jump a little. She swallowed the last bite of the cookie and gulped some tea. "Who's at the door?" Thea asked, addressing her cabin's AI.

"Beatrice Miller is waiting to talk to you," the AI replied.

Thea hesitated a moment, not sure if she felt like company. "Open the door," Thea said, realizing she might be able to get some ideas from Beatrice and refocus her investigation.

"My dear, I've been looking everywhere for you." Beatrice bustled into the room with her cloud of white hair and took a seat opposite Thea. "I happen to know that you heard everything Lottie said a couple of days ago, and I want to be the first to apologize for her words. They were completely uncalled for. I don't really know what's got into her; she's usually such a kind soul."

"It seemed that way when I first met her," Thea said, "but now I'm not so sure. She just seems determined to hate me, and I don't understand why."

"Yes, well, that is unfortunate," Beatrice said, rearranging her feet and turning away from Thea.

"What aren't you telling me?" Thea asked, sitting up straight.

"Well, really, you already know what the problem is," Beatrice said. "They're basically afraid of the fact that you're an Askovian."

Thea crossed her arms, narrowing her eyes. "So, why are you here?"

"As to that," Beatrice said, "Jemma and I have been working on the funeral arrangements for poor Imogen. It's meant to be a private ceremony, but there's a disagreement among us. It seems Jemma wants to invite you, and..."

"Lottie doesn't..." Thea said with a cheerless laugh. "It's alright; I really didn't want to go, anyway. I hardly knew Imogen, and I was only starting to get to know Jemma. But I don't want to be anywhere near Lottie."

"I don't think it's fair to say that you hardly knew Imogen," Beatrice said. "We were all getting to know each other. And if there had been more time, you two would've become good friends."

"I think that's the point," Thea said. "We didn't have very much time together. For example, I didn't know Imogen was so wealthy."

"Where did you hear that?" Beatrice asked.

"Captain Ebert," Thea said.

"Oh, of course," Beatrice said. "Those two went back a long way. But you're right; Imogen inherited a lot of credits because she was a Viewer. Although her abilities were weak, she still received training at Heliton. Also, she donated a lot of it to charity, but there are still millions of credits left. I suspect it'll go to the cousins on her mom's side, though."

"Is Jemma related to her on her mom's side?" Thea asked.

"No, on her dad's," Beatrice said.

"I see," Thea said. "I was just wondering if there was maybe some sort of motive."

"For Jemma to murder Imogen?" Beatrice said with one raised eyebrow. "She would never do that to her aunt. Okay, she wasn't exactly Jemma's aunt, but they were very close."

Thea contemplated the coffee table as her shoulders drooped.

"My dear," Beatrice began, waiting for Thea to face her. "Do you have any friends on board the ship?"

"Well," Thea said, pausing. "I have classmates in Alice's class. We sometimes meet for meals. But usually, we discuss events from the class, which is the main thing we have in common."

"I worry about you," Beatrice said. "You seemed to have formed a friendship with Lottie and Jemma at the beginning of our trip. But now they've both cooled toward you, and eight months is a long time to go with no friends."

"I made a huge mistake leaving Earth," Thea said, sinking further into her chair. "I had lots of friends, and I even had a cushy job waiting for me."

"Why did you leave?" Beatrice asked softly.

"The thrill of adventure," Thea said with a lopsided smile. "Brimble Mining offered me my dream job, and I couldn't pass it up."

"What is your dream job?" Beatrice asked, activating the crafter. A moment later, a warm cup of tea materialized on the coffee table.

"I want to be a farmer," Thea said as her cheeks grew warm. "I know that sounds crazy, but I like everything about growing plants. I like developing new species, creating new devices to keep them safe, and adjusting their nutrition yields for our benefit."

"Sounds like a true Romly farmer," Beatrice said with an encouraging smile. "Why not go back to Anteros and join the family farm?"

Because they don't want me, she thought. Thea flinched at the mention of her family's name. Then she shrugged a shoulder.

Beatrice took a sip of tea, waiting for Thea's answer.

"Anyway, I can't focus on that right now," Thea said in a quiet voice. "I have to find the killer before he or she strikes again."

CHAPTER 16

Later that night, Thea, dressed in her pajamas, combed through the Net looking for the Anteros Gazette; it was a popular gossip site mostly focused on the lives of the Askovs. She found the gazette and, with her lips set in a grim line, launched her fact-finding mission. Beginning with a general search for Imogen Stone, Thea munched on a small stack of buttered cookies and swallowed a little hot tea. She stumbled across a huge number of articles from about two years ago. Settling in, she began reading as a small scandal unfolded. Thea paused with her cup halfway to her mouth at some of the unbelievable events.

"No!" Thea said, replacing her cup on the table with a snap. She was surprised at the vitriol from the people involved. Why wasn't the IPS involved sooner? Once she completed her research, a new idea crossed Thea's mind. She couldn't speak to Jemma or Lottie any longer but wondered if Owen would be open to talking to her. She debated the best way to do this because she wasn't sure if Owen still blamed her for his wife's death. After an internal debate, she realized she might be able to save another life and sent the following message:

Hello Owen,

I hope this finds you well. I would like to understand better what happened to your wife, Veronica, and, more recently, to Imogen. You don't have any reason to trust me, but I'd really like to find the killer before he or she takes another life. Would you be willing to help me?

Thea

After sending the message, a huge yawn escaped her lips as she hoped to meet him in the next couple of days.

The following morning, Thea rose early, showered, and selected a steaming cup of coffee with toast. As she munched on her food, she noticed that she had received a response from Owen.

Hello Thea,

I've wanted to talk to you for a couple of weeks now. There are so many things I would like to discuss with you. Would you be open to meeting me in my cabin sometime this morning?

Owen

Thea paused, not because she didn't want to meet Owen, but because she wasn't sure meeting him in his cabin was very smart. She munched on a second bite of toast while she debated her options. Maybe it would be better in his cabin for privacy. If he tried something, she could use her Mover abilities to protect herself. Intrigued, she looked forward to hearing what he had to say after wanting to talk to her for two weeks.

Finishing the last of her coffee, she replied to Owen, saying she'd meet him in forty-five minutes.

Later, Thea walked to Owen's cabin, which was on the same floor as hers. She gently knocked, and the door immediately slid open.

"Come in, come in!" Owen said, making his way to the door. He was in his early thirties and, like his sister Lottie, he had black wavy hair and lightly tanned skin.

"I'm so glad you could make it," Owen said with a genial grin. "Please come and have a seat."

Thea made her way to one of the overstuffed chairs opposite the sofa. Owen settled onto the sofa opposite her.

"Would you like something to drink?" He gestured to the meal crafter on the coffee table between them.

"I've just had breakfast," Thea said, shaking her head.

"So, how have you been?" Owen asked. "I understand there was an attempt made on your life earlier."

"I'm okay," Thea said, perplexed by his friendly demeanor. "Sorry, but the last time we spoke, you accused me of murder. What's changed?"

Owen's face turned pink as he stared at the coffee table. He shifted uncomfortably on the sofa and appeared to be gathering his thoughts.

"You're right," he said in a quiet voice. "When we first met, I'd just learned my wife had passed away, and I was just too...emotional. I took it out on you, and I'm very sorry for that. It wasn't your fault, and I've felt guilty about it ever since. I was also too embarrassed to apologize, but I'm glad you contacted me."

"Well, I'm very sorry for your loss," Thea said.

"Thank you," Owen said with a nod.

"Even if you don't hate me, your sister certainly does," Thea said with a small smile.

"Oh, that..." Owen said with a chuckle as he nervously adjusted his collar. "It's true; when we were all younger, we were bullied by very powerful Askovians. In our case, they were Readers. I understand from Charlotte that you're Askovian, too, but you're a Mover. I know you've never done anything to harm them. Also, I personally think they're all overreacting. I'm sorry for your poor treatment."

Thea gazed at him, surprised at the heavy feeling that lifted off her shoulders. Her ex-friends had accused her of something she'd never done, and she had no way of proving her innocence. But with Owen's words, she could start letting go, which made her feel better.

"What did you want to talk to me about?" Owen asked.

"I've been digging into Imogen's past," Thea said. "I stumbled across the Anteros Gazette, and I just wondered if you could shed more light on what I found there."

"But that's just a gossip site," Owen said with a smirk. "I don't think you can trust anything you find there."

"I think it's generally truthful, but it's very light on details," Thea said.

"Yeah, they do that so they don't get sued," Owen said, chuckling. "But since they're so vague, they can also insinuate wrong information."

"That's true," Thea said. "And that's partly what I want to talk to you about. So, this has to do with a scandal that erupted about two years ago but really began around fifteen years prior. When my siblings, Mara and Noah, were in their teens, they were friends with your family, the Gothams, and their cousins, the Stones, who were all very advanced Readers. I only vaguely remembered my brother and sister mentioning something about this, but I was only around five years old."

"I know the event you're talking about," Owen said in a dark tone. "We were being plagued by the Stone cousins." He laughed harshly. "Veronica, who was also a Reader, was nothing like those cousins. Her abilities were very weak, and she was a very kind soul."

"You're right," Thea said. "The Stones had systematically bullied many non-Askovians, including Originals as well as Askovs without abilities. They'd caused multiple injuries requiring overnight stays in fully equipped hospitals. The IPS had been involved but never brought any charges against Readers."

Surprised, Mara and Noah weren't involved in the bullying, she thought. Her brother and sister loved to bully her, but then she realized that these were Readers, and her siblings may not have been able to defend themselves.

"Yeah, the worst thing about all of it was the cover-up," Owen said. "Their parents put a lot of pressure on the IPS to keep it from becoming public knowledge. At the same time, they arranged to have the injured kids taken care of using the best medical technology had to offer. Only their parents had to agree not to press charges and not to publicize what their children had done. After the first couple of incidents, your parents kept your brother and sister away from us. It was a smart move."

"It seems the news about all of this only surfaced two years ago," Thea said. "The most noticeable thing about all of these articles was Imogen's hard stance against her own cousins. She'd been the one to condemn their behavior. Even though Imogen was family, she couldn't ignore their behavior."

"There must be something that the three of us have in common," Thea said with wrinkled eyebrows.

"Maybe it was that you were all Askovian," Owen said, running a hand through his hair.

"I don't think that's it," Thea said with a frustrated huff. "I wish I could just figure this out. In any case, Imogen made a final public statement. She cut off her cousins. Do you know what that meant?"

"My understanding is she changed her will," Owen said, rubbing his forehead. "Right now, I can't remember, though, if she named her new beneficiaries."

"I was hoping you'd have the answer to that one too," Thea said and then turned to the crafter. "Would you mind if I have a glass of water?"

Owen leaned toward the crafter and selected a glass of water, which materialized directly in front of Thea.

"I also researched your wife, Veronica," Thea said after taking a sip of water. "I can't find any evidence that there was anything to inherit from her mom."

"Unfortunately, or fortunately, I happen to visit Petra while my wife..." Owen said, flexing his fist. "I had to explain that someone sent a message that the party moved to Petra's cabin. Then, I had to explain multiple times to those idiots in the IPS that I didn't get anything from Veronica's death. Finally, I waited several days while they tried to contact Earth to verify everything."

"Was there any evidence of the message?" Thea asked.

"No," Owen said with an edge to his voice. "Someone wanted to make it look like I killed her because of Petra."

"Strange, but they also gave you an alibi. Do you have any enemies?"

"Not to my knowledge. I've accidentally irritated people in the past, but nothing that would make them want to murder me."

"What happened to Veronica's family?" Thea asked. "I couldn't find anything."

"The entire family declared bankruptcy just a few months ago," Owen said. "They had mismanaged all of their businesses and properties. Veronica would've never gotten anything."

A moment of silence passed between them.

"How are things going with the funeral?" Thea asked.

He shook his head. "I'm getting close to getting permission to organize her funeral."

"Do you need help?" Thea asked, drinking water.

"No, Jemma and Lottie are both helping," Owen said. "But of course, Jemma and Sam are now busy with Imogen."

"What about those two?" Thea asked. "Are they able to inherit from Imogen?"

"I don't think so," he said. "Imogen's inheritance came to her with very specific terms because she had no children. There are details about who qualifies as a beneficiary, who can get the credits or property, and more. One of those Stone cousins would know more. Also, I understand the attorneys are threatening to sue the Stargazers' corporate owners for negligence. That means the attorneys have to get paid. In the end, there may be no inheritance left." He set his lips in a straight line.

Even though Owen had said there was no way Jemma could inherit it, she wanted to ask her in person. Thea made a mental note to send her a quick message after she finished her talk with Owen.

About an hour and a half later, Thea made her way to one of the ship's pools while her mind ran in circles, trying to figure out the killer's identity. She needed a change and had chosen the one that was a little out of the way for most adults because she liked the solitude. Once there, she removed her clothes, revealing her swimsuit, and dove headfirst into the water. She loved the exhilarating feeling of the cold water wrapping around her body. The bubbles rubbed against her skin as she started to make her way to the surface, which left her feeling exhilarated. Finally, when her face broke through the water, and she took in her first big breath, suddenly everything in the world felt right, and a broad smile covered her face.

She looked at the opposite end of the pool and swam with powerful strokes in that direction. Sometimes, exerting a lot of energy helped her to think through problems. Once she'd finished four laps, she pulled herself out at the edge as her auburn hair became plastered to her head. Raising her hands high in the air with her arms still straight, she touched her toes. Something about that stretch also left her invigorated. She stepped to the lounge chair where she'd left her belongings and wrapped herself in a towel. After taking a sip of fizzy pink lemonade, she sent a message to Jemma, offering condolences and asking who would inherit from Imogen. Scanning her message again, she hoped that it had been sensitive enough for the circumstances while at the same time conveying that she really was trying to help.

Sighing, she realized Jemma might not answer because of their non-friendship. Thea sent the message and leaned back in her chair, wrapped in a cozy towel, thinking of the next steps in her investigation.

CHAPTER 17

Sometime in the middle of the night, Thea felt the cold air on her back and legs. Still groggy from sleep, she tried to open her eyes, but her lids were heavy and wouldn't lift. She shivered at the cold metal across her upper back and under her knees. After a moment, she realized she wasn't in bed anymore. The realization made her eyes pop open.

She still wore her comfy sage pajamas, but her shirt rode up on her back, and the pants exposed her lower legs. Gazing at her surroundings, she noticed a gray corridor that could honestly be anywhere on the Stargazer. She turned to the side and nearly screamed at the metallic robot's face, carrying her in the middle of the night. That explained the metal across her back and under her knees.

What am I doing here? What's going on?

She tried to wriggle out of its arms, but it tightened his grip.

"Put me down," Thea said, trying to keep the panic out of her voice.

The robot didn't respond and continued to walk down the deserted, gray corridor.

"I said, put me down now!" Thea shouted. "Stop!"

The robot never slowed and didn't acknowledge her, but Thea thought she recognized it.

"Who are you?" Thea asked, doing her best to keep her emotions in check. Her heart hammered in her chest as she examined the robot. It looked like the same one used by the IPS during Imogen's death.

The robot didn't respond.

Thea realized somebody else was controlling this robot. She wondered if they monitored her, too. She twisted and turned harder within its arms and managed to scoot one leg out of its hold. Her head felt fuzzy as she struggled to think, and somehow, movement made things worse.

The robot never slowed, and it never turned toward her. That's when she realized whoever controlled the robot couldn't actually observe her.

I might have a chance of escaping, she thought.

A moment later, the robot entered a large set of double doors, pacing into a quiet room filled with gadgets. From school, she recognized the devices used to measure an engine's efficiency, monitor crystal fuel purity, and perform regular maintenance.

"Where am I?" Thea asked, but she knew from studying the Stargazer, it was the Engineering Instrumentation room. "Where are you taking me?"

The robot continued walking until it reached a second set of double doors. Thea's eyes widened. "No! I command you to stop!" she yelled. These doors led to one of the ship's many airlocks. A frisson of fear raced down her spine, and Thea worked harder to get out of the robot's arms. The effort temporarily increased the foggy feeling, but she knew she couldn't stop.

She twisted harder, freeing her second leg, which caused both feet to thump onto the floor. However, the robot had tightened one arm around her torso, and now she was trapped next to it. She used that moment to catch her breath and organize her thoughts.

With its free arm, the robot activated the controls to the airlock, causing the doors to slide open. Stale air washed over Thea, and she knew she had to fight. Thea forced her legs across both doors to prevent the robot from entering. It effortlessly shoved her into the center of the chamber, the doors slid shut, and the room swam as she fought the slowness in her mind.

"Let me out of here!" Thea shouted. With her auburn hair on her face, she scampered to the door's edge, frantically looking for the controls. The effort left her huffing for air. If she couldn't figure out how to open the door, she would be in trouble. Just as that thought crossed her mind, the Engineering AI issued a lengthy warning about initiating a countdown to the airlock doors opening. She saw a line of ten red-lit squares, one of them blinking. How long had that been flickering on and off?

"Ten," the AI said as the tenth light blinked on and off.

Think, Thea, think. She forced herself to organize her thoughts.

Frantically running her hands along the wall, she searched for any sort of emergency button that might be near those countdown lights. She turned to the doors facing space and ran her hands along that door as well.

"Nothing!" she said, rubbing her face and trying to get rid of that foggy feeling. "What am I going to do?"

She turned to the wall on the left and found it suspiciously clear of any buttons or screens. She pressed her fingers at random points along the wall but found nothing.

"Nine," the AI said, and the tenth light went black while the ninth one flickered off and on.

Thea looked at the doors leading back to the Instrumentation room. A large window dominated both doors, and there were no buttons on the doors or the surrounding walls. She trembled as she realized she was out of ideas.

"No, no, I'm not giving up," she said, taking a deep breath to steady her nerves.

She examined the walls above the doors and found nothing. But when she ran her hands down the wall framing the right door, she felt something give way. She continued running her hands along the door and found nothing else.

"Eight," the AI said, and the ninth light shut off while the eighth light blinked.

Sweat beaded on her forehead as she felt a tightness grip her chest. She ran her hands along the wall next to the left door. It was completely smooth, except for one area that gave way when her fingers ran over it. She turned to the other soft spot on the right door and noticed that they were at the exact same height but on either side of the door. This gave her hope that these were emergency buttons to open the doors.

Glancing at the window, Thea noted that the robot was no longer by the window. She peeked through the window and noticed it wasn't even in the room. She decided to take her chances and fully pressed what she presumed to be an emergency button on the left side of the door.

"Nothing!" she said. "How could it be nothing?"

"Seven," the AI said, and the eighth light darkened while the seventh flickered on and off.

Thea frantically raced to the right side of the door and punched that button. The murky feeling clouded her mind, but only for a moment. None of the doors budged, and the countdown light continued blinking. After a moment of frustration, she scanned the ceiling, but it was completely smooth. Then, she examined the carpeted floor.

"Maybe there's something under here," she said.

After unsuccessfully trying to pull up the carpet, she stepped to the double doors leading to the Instrumentation room. She went back to both buttons along the doors and pressed them one after the other, hoping it would eventually work.

"Wait a minute," she said. "The robot didn't respond to voice commands. Clearly, the killer had augmented it. Did he also disable the emergency buttons in the airlock's doors? I'll have to use the emergency buttons on the other side."

"Six," the AI said, and the seventh light went out while the sixth one fluttered on and off.

"Where are the exterior emergencies?" she asked, looking through the door's window into the Engineering room. Hoping she'd see something to help her, she surveyed the room and found another airlock on the other side.

"There it is!" Thea yelled excitedly. The two must have the same emergency handles.

Normally, Movers needed to see what they were trying to manipulate. In this case, Thea had to use what she saw of the chamber across the room and a little of her imagination. She took a deep breath and centered herself while she studied the location of the emergency handle on the other cell.

"Five," the AI said, and the sixth light disappeared while the fifth switched on and off.

Thea shook as she peeked at the door leading to space.

"Pull yourself together," she said in a harsh voice while forcing herself to concentrate.

Then she used her ability to probe the outside of her airlock. It was a slow process. She started at the top of the wall and slowly worked her way down until she sensed a difference in depth. She presumed that was the location of the pull and used her Mover abilities to yank as hard as she could.

"No, no, no!" Thea yelled. "Why isn't this working?"

She groaned as she realized the killer had disabled the emergencies on both sides of the airlock doors. In frustration, she resumed her pounding on the door. "Help!" she cried.

"Four," the AI said, and the fifth light went out while the fourth one flashed on and off.

"Think," she said, running her fingers through her hair as she paced in a circle.

A moment later, a new thought crossed her mind. Why did the killer disable the emergency system? To prevent anyone from being alerted.

Thea raced back to the window and peered at the emergency pulls on the opposite airlock's doors, and then a small smile crept across her face.

"Three," the AI said, and the fourth light went black while the third one blinked.

Thea's smile immediately disappeared as she focused her mind and pulled the emergency cord as hard as she could on the other chamber doors.

The entire room lit up with flashing red lights.

"Emergency," the ship's AI said. "All passengers remain where you are. In case of sudden decompression, bulkhead doors will activate for your protection."

She couldn't hear the countdown any longer and hoped she wasn't in for a nasty surprise.

A moment later, several crew members streamed into the Engineering Instrumentation room. Thea banged on the door, knowing they couldn't hear her, but hoped they'd notice the movement behind the glass.

It worked; a young crew member in a blue uniform noticed and dashed to her door. He tried to deactivate the lock, but the door remained closed. Ulrick, the Science Officer, and Quincy, the Navigation Officer, joined him. Together, they struggled to open the door, repeatedly pressing a button, and she wondered if they were trying the intercom.

She pointed at the countdown, which was now on 'one,' and Ulrick selected something on his comm. Suddenly, the lights turned off, and she began to float.

Thea screamed. The sudden loss of gravity made her think Ulrick had accidentally opened the door to space. A moment later, she realized he'd simply cut the power in the airlock.

Glancing at the countdown, she verified it had stopped. All of the lights were dark, and thankfully, the doors leading to the vacuum hadn't opened.

Several more crew members joined them. They appeared to be discussing something, but she couldn't hear a thing. After waiting while some crew members tinkered with the door, the lights came back on, and she crashed to the floor, smacking her head against the carpet.

"Thea!" Dr. Hadley said, rushing through the airlock's doors. She held a small scanner and ran it over Thea's body. "Are you injured?"

Pure joy flooded Thea's body, causing her eyes to tear up, and then everything went dark.

CHAPTER 18

Thea woke much later that morning with a sharp headache. She groaned as she turned her head, and her stomach tightened with nausea. With steadying breaths, her queasiness disappeared, and her eyes slowly fluttered open.

"I see you're awake," Dr. Hadley said with a gentle smile. "It seems you received a heavy dose of a sedative. In fact, I have no idea why you ever woke up."

Rubbing her temples, she recognized the ship's infirmary. Thea struggled to recall the previous night's events, and slowly, her memory floated into focus. "Oh, I think I'm starting to remember." She winced at a spike of pain.

"Yeah, it might take a few more minutes for everything to come back to you," Dr. Hadley said. "That particular sedative causes temporary memory loss, but just for a couple of minutes. The real side effect is the splitting headache. How do you feel?"

"Like my head is about to come apart," Thea said in a hoarse voice. "Can you give me something for it?" She normally didn't like to take medication, but the pain was so intense she was open to anything the doctor could offer.

"Of course, let me give it to you right now," Dr. Hadley said, selecting some buttons on a floating screen. The medipad's nanobots immediately dispensed the painkiller, and a couple of minutes later, Thea's face relaxed as the pain subsided.

"How much do you remember about last night?" Dr. Hadley asked.

"Let me see...that metal robot was carrying me somewhere," Thea said, struggling to sit upright on the medipad.

"I don't think you should sit up yet," Dr. Hadley said. "Even though the sedative has worn off, your body is still coping with the side effects."

"I feel better upright," Thea said, scooting her legs off the floating bed and taking a deep breath.

Dr. Hadley adjusted the floating bed so that a backrest extended from a hidden compartment to support Thea.

"Let's see," Thea said. "The robot deposited me in some kind of airlock. There was a countdown. I think that's what really woke me up. I was terrified I was going to die. Even though my head was so fuzzy, I knew I couldn't give in."

"Well, no doubt the IPS will be here to question you in more detail," Dr. Hadley said. "I'm just glad you figured out how to save yourself."

The door to the infirmary chimed.

"Who is at the door?" Dr. Hadley asked the infirmary's AI, turning to the door.

"Jemma Gotham is waiting to see Thea Black," the AI said.

"Are you up for a visitor?" Dr. Hadley asked with a questioning look.

"Sure," Thea said as a huge knot tightened in her chest. "I'm just a little surprised."

A moment later, Jemma burst into the room and dashed straight to Thea. She enveloped Thea in a hug. "I can't believe this has happened to you," Jemma's voice quivered. "I let my brother and Lottie talk me into believing you were the killer. But you were just another victim. This is the second time the killer has actually gone after you. I'm so sorry I wasn't there to help you."

"You realize there was nothing you could've done last night?" Thea said as the knot in her chest unwound and disappeared. It was so wonderful to have the support of at least one friend.

"Well, probably not in the middle of the night," Jemma said. "But I could've supported you before that. I basically didn't want to go against Sam and Lottie, so I just went along with what they were saying. But Owen cornered us yesterday and told us everything you two had discussed. And that made me feel bad about how I treated you. I'm really sorry."

"Well, don't be sorry now," Thea said with a lopsided smile. "Instead, try to figure out how to sneak me out of here," she whispered loudly.

"You're not going anywhere until I finish my final exam," Dr. Hadley said with a small smile.

"So, are you up for telling me what happened last night?" Jemma asked with halting words.

"Yeah, I had just started telling Dr. Hadley," Thea said as she recounted everything she'd already mentioned to the doctor. "Once I was in the airlock, I tried desperately to find an emergency exit button. It took me a while to realize that I had found both buttons, but they were disabled."

"Wow, that must've been so scary," Jemma said, squeezing Thea's hand. "But how did you get out of there?"

The door to the infirmary chimed again.

"Open," Dr. Hadley said without even asking the AI who was there.

Agent Walker stepped into the room with furrowed eyebrows. He peered at all three women before settling on Thea. "How are you this morning? Are you up for any questions?"

"Yes, I think so," Thea said. "As long as it doesn't take too long."

"It won't," Agent Walker said. "I just need to perform a preliminary interview." He created a floating screen set to private and selected some buttons that Thea couldn't see. He turned to face Thea. "Do you consent to being recorded?"

"Yes," Thea said, settling into the makeshift seat created by the floating medipad.

"Would you tell me in as much detail as possible exactly what happened to you last night?" Agent Walker asked.

Thea recounted everything she had told Jemma. "Then I realized that even though my airlock was disabled, the empty chamber across from me was not, and I hoped the killer hadn't disabled the alarm. Finally, I activated the empty airlock."

"At any point were you able to communicate with the robot?" Agent Walker asked, adding some notes to his floating screen.

"No, it never acknowledged me," Thea said. "Well, one time it did; when I nearly squeezed out of its grasp, it tightened its hold on me. After that, it left the Instrumentation room, so I think somebody else was controlling it, but I don't really know."

"Dr. Hadley's preliminary report states you had a strong sedative in your system," Agent Walker said. "What did you have last night?"

"I just had my normal evening tea with some butter cookies," Thea said. "I've eaten that many times if I'm staying up late to get something done."

"Interesting," Agent Walker said, running a hand through his wavy blond hair. "We checked your pantry. It wasn't tampered with. So we're not sure how the sedative got into your system."

"But there was so much sedative," Dr. Hadley said, her face pinched. "I just don't think it could've been administered through food. Also, given the dose, I have no idea why Thea even woke up."

"I think fear will do that to you," Thea said with a frown. "In my sleep, my back became icy cold. I tried to turn over and pull up the blanket when I noticed I couldn't. More time went by before I realized I couldn't move my legs or arms, which made me panic. When my eyes finally popped open, I noticed not only was I not in bed, but I wasn't in my room. Instead, a metal creature was carrying me. I was still having trouble thinking; my head was so hazy and terrified."

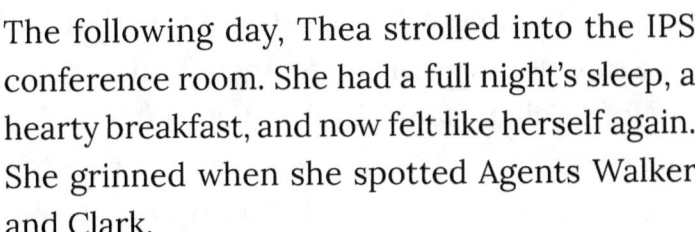

The following day, Thea strolled into the IPS conference room. She had a full night's sleep, a hearty breakfast, and now felt like herself again. She grinned when she spotted Agents Walker and Clark.

"Good morning, Ms. Black," Agent Clark said, her brown hair in a tight ponytail. "Please have a seat." She indicated the chair opposite.

"Dr. Hadley informs us the side effects of the sedative should be completely worn off by now," Agent Walker said. "How are you feeling?"

"Fine," Thea said, shrugging one shoulder. "This is the best I've felt since boarding this ship. If it weren't for the fact that somebody was trying to murder me, I'd say this has been a good cruise." She intended that to be a little joke, but nobody laughed.

"If you don't mind, we'd like to ask more detailed questions," Agent Walker said.

The door slid open, and Captain Ebert rushed into the room, grabbing the chair next to Thea. "How are you this morning?" the captain asked.

"Very good," Thea said. "I'm especially happy to be alive."

"No doubt," he half-smiled. "I hope I haven't missed much." He turned to Agent Walker.

"No," Walker said. "We've just started." He turned to Thea. "We all reviewed your statement, and we have some follow-up questions. Can you give us a more detailed description of the robot that held you?"

"It was similar to the robot you used when Imogen died," Thea said, staring down at the desk as if trying to gather her thoughts. "It had that bland metal face, sharp contours for the arms and legs, but a smooth torso. Also, it wasn't exactly the same shade of gray metal. The contours on the arms and legs were darker shades of gray. I suppose it has tools or even weapons inside its arms and legs."

Agent Walker and Clark exchanged glances.

"What I don't understand is why there's no record of a robot having any sort of excursion last night," Captain Ebert said. "There isn't even a record of you and the robot walking from your cabin to the Instrumentation room."

"We'll get to that in a moment," Agent Clark said. "We have another question first. Would you tell us again the last thing you ate last night?"

"Hot tea with lots of milk," Thea said, glancing at the ceiling to jog her memory. "And a couple or... four soft butter cookies."

"You see, I told you that's too little food to administer that sedative," Agent Clark said, turning to Walker.

"I also had my doubts about that," Ebert said, his eyebrows wrinkled. "The killer used something else to administer that much sedative."

"Now that I think about it," Thea said, scratching her head, "the murderer could've administered the sedative through my pantry but maybe only contaminated one item. After that, it'd be easier to remove the evidence. But a second option would be to have the robot administer it."

"I thought of that too," Agent Walker said. "But the AI would've alerted you if someone opened your door."

"Maybe, maybe not," Captain Ebert said. "Considering the amount of tampering involved, the killer could've disabled the cabin's alarm."

Thea shivered, realizing how vulnerable she'd been last night.

"Now, the surveillance vids," Agent Walker said. "The surprising thing about disabling the vids is it requires access to several different ship systems. Disabling the vids in the walkways requires Operations. Disabling the vids inside the lift is Engineering. Finally, in the Instrumentation room, that obviously is Engineering again." He paused and analyzed each of their faces as if he wanted them to understand something. "But the airlock is the most telling piece of evidence. It requires a combination of Medical and Command. Do you know what that means?"

"Yes, unfortunately, I do," Captain Ebert said in a heavy voice. "One of my crew is responsible for this." His lips formed a grim line.

"That's why we invited you here," Agent Walker said. "Can you narrow down who'd have that level of access, especially the command?"

"This does narrow things down a little," the captain said. "But it only narrows it down to maybe six crew members, including myself."

"Would you provide us with a list of the names?" Clark asked. "That way, we can get started with interviews?"

Ebert nodded, his face set in a scowl.

"I understand you don't want to believe that anybody you handpicked to work on your ship could be guilty." Walker's eyes bored into Ebert's. "But people are dying; we need to get to the bottom of this quickly."

"I agree," Ebert said and sighed. "I just can't believe we've come to this point."

"On a different note," Thea said. "Can we talk about Veronica's murder?"

"Of course," Walker said with a steady gaze.

"When Veronica was murdered," Thea said. "There was an emergency that canceled the crew's party. Do you know what it was?"

"Yes, a faulty indicator in one of the engineering airlocks," Walker said. "Unfortunately, it took them hours to track down the cause and then implement the solution."

"Doesn't that seem a little coincidental?" Thea said. "I mean, maybe this can narrow the list further."

"Not really," Ebert said. "The same six people would've had access to that system too."

Thea stared down at the table, wondering who could be behind the murders and attempt on her life.

"One last thing," Agent Walker asked, breaking into Thea's thoughts. "On a hunch, we searched through our database and compared it with the Heliton Academy version. Someone altered several elements in your records. Now, the alterations aren't permanent in that we haven't synced with the Earth database yet. But that level of tampering is also part of Command. What we can't figure out is why the killer would even need to do that. He, or maybe she, had initially erased any information related to your Askovian abilities, but we've returned to the Heliton version."

Thea's mind whirled with the numerous accusations she'd faced recently about hiding her abilities, and she wondered if it was relevant.

CHAPTER 19

After talking with the IPS, Thea stepped into the lift, intending to return to her cabin. Her stomach rumbled loudly as she stepped out of the antigrav lifts on her floor. She began thinking of what she'd like for lunch, but loud, chaotic noises distracted her—they sounded like people celebrating in the courtyard. Curious, she changed direction and instead headed toward the courtyard.

"Alice!" Thea shouted, and a broad grin spread across her face. She raced to the center of the crowd and joined in the giant group hug that had developed around Alice. It was rare to see Alice laughing and returning affection towards her friends, but this was a special occasion.

"I'm so glad those stupid IPS agents figured out you were innocent," Fiona said and chuckled.

"But it took them so long to figure it out," Dessie said. "I wonder if we should start working on suing them."

"No, I'm not suing anybody," Alice said. "But I'm happy to be out of there."

"And we're all extremely happy to have you back," Beatrice said with a warm smile.

"Alice, I've missed you and your amazing classes," Thea said. "After you rest up, we have to get started again. I have so many questions."

"I can't wait to get back to my classes," Alice said, looking around at the crowd. "But right now, I am really hungry. Can we have lunch?"

Immediately, the group assembled several tables and chairs together to create one giant rectangular table with chairs lining both sides. Alice sat at the head of the table with her friends nearby, acting like a shield. Thea sat between Beatrice and Jemma while a number of other friends filled out the rest of the giant makeshift table. But Thea noticed Lottie and Sam at the very end of the table. Thea's and Lottie's eyes met before she turned to her brother.

"Don't mind them," Jemma said in a low voice. "They're never going to accept you. It's best if you just ignore them."

"I know...you're right," Thea said and sighed.

"You know what I've been craving lately?" Alice asked, laughing.

"Yeah!" Beatrice said, nodding her head. This produced a few titters among the other ladies.

"Time for stinky meat!" Fiona announced loudly while making a selection on the nearest meal crafter. Everybody laughed. A moment later, a plate of warm jellied meat, consisting of a mixture of various mystery meat products aged over a period of weeks, appeared in front of everyone. It had a very distinct flavor that natives of Anteros loved, but newcomers intensely disliked. It was always served with a mountain of either mashed potatoes or rice and tiny green flowered vegetables, also native to Anteros. Generally, children liked the stronger taste of the meal and enjoyed it their entire lives. People moving to Anteros as adults had no tolerance for the strong smell and taste. This time, though, there were no non-Anteros passengers at the table.

"So what's it like being in the ship's prison?" Dessie asked, drinking some beet juice.

"It wasn't so different from being here," Alice said, swallowing the last bite of her lunch. "I mostly spent my time in a cabin locked away from everybody else, but I had a chance to read.

And every evening, the captain escorted me to the crew's dining room where I ate with them. They discussed matters about the ship, which was a little boring. But there are one or two things I happened to pick up."

"Did you hear anything about the murders from the crew's point of view?" Thea asked, leaning in.

"Oh my dear, I only recently heard what happened to you," Alice said, standing up, pacing to Thea, and giving her a quick hug. "Are you okay, my dear?"

Thea nodded, unable to respond. It wasn't often she felt so welcomed and part of the community. A moment later, Alice took her seat and carefully gazed at the remaining people at the table. "Have you thought about what type of person could be behind this?"

"Actually, we have," Fiona said, turning to Dessie and Beatrice. "Initially, we thought this was some crazy person. Now it's clear there's no insanity here. The only thing is there's no clear goal—otherwise, why go after Thea twice?"

"I completely agree with you," Alice said. "Why go after her twice?" She emphasized the last word. "I've been pondering this for the last few hours, but I can't come up with an answer for it."

"Well, for now, let's focus on welcoming you back," Thea said, desperately trying to change the subject so she wouldn't be the center of attention. This actually worked, and Fiona, Dessie, and Beatrice took up the conversation again, asking Alice about resuming her classes and any plans she had for the coming eight months until they reached Anteros. Thea relaxed a little as she enjoyed the conversation swirling around her. Out of the corner of her eye, she saw Lottie leave with her brother. She wondered why they had even bothered to show up.

In the middle of the afternoon, Thea walked to Alice's cabin. She ran through her questions for the ladies as an air of determination settled on her. As she stepped through the doors, she smiled her greetings to Beatrice, who held up a glass of Anteros wine.

"Do you want one?" Beatrice asked, taking a sip of wine.

"No," Thea said, shaking her head. "But I will have a cup of coffee. Where's Alice?" Thea took a seat in one of the overstuffed chairs across from Beatrice. A large floating screen hovered over the coffee table between them.

"I'm right here," Alice said, stepping out of her bedroom and sitting on the sofa next to Beatrice. Alice adjusted the floating screen, which showed her lesson plan for her Astronomy class.

"I'm just getting ready for my next few sets of classes," Alice said. "Did you know we can do virtual tunneling into some asteroids drifting near us?"

"Virtual tunneling?" Thea asked, momentarily distracted from her purpose. "Does that mean you scan the asteroid and determine exactly what's in it?"

"Yes, that's exactly it," Alice said enthusiastically. "There are so many things we've discovered about the occasional asteroid. Many of them have similar cores. This supports one theory that they all came from the same body, probably millions or billions of years ago. I wonder what our solar system looked like back then?"

"I know. Sometimes I wish I had a time machine," Thea said with a small chuckle. Then she remembered her mission. "So the reason I wanted to meet was to discuss my investigation. So far I'm a little stuck. There are three possible motives to kill me: credits, political power, and love. I eliminated the last one because I'm not in love with anyone, and no one feels that way about me. My family appears wealthy because of our farm, but our business runs with very low margins. We also have limited political powers."

"What would you like to know?" Beatrice asked, swallowing more wine.

"I know the captain prepared a list of possible suspects for the IPS," Thea said, running both hands through her auburn hair. "It's based on the senior crew members, even though I can't imagine why any of them would want to harm me."

"I heard Captain Ebert talking about the list of crew members who could've done that to you," Alice said. "He mentioned it'd take Command permissions, which includes him, but also involves the heads of every department—Communications, Operations, Navigation, Science, and Engineering."

"I propose we do a deep dive into each one of those people," Thea said. "I'm a little hesitant because I've met all of those people, and I'm not even related to them. They have no reason to want me dead, and they'd literally gain nothing."

"I spent quite a bit of time with the captain," Beatrice said. "I know that crew fairly well."

"Let's just take them one by one," Thea said.

"The head of Communications is Kroft," Beatrice said. "She's Askov with no abilities, but she was born and raised in Tymal and only makes these trips as part of her job."

"Do we have access to Earth's Net?" Thea asked.

"Yes, that's why I brought this up," Alice said, changing the view on her floating screen to show Kroft's known information on the Net. "She comes from a family of Listeners. No member of this family is related directly to you. In other words, if you pass away, they'd inherit nothing from you. As far as I can tell, you've never even met them, but you did go to school with a cousin. The family doesn't appear to have political ambitions. In short, I can't see any link between you and Kroft."

"Interesting," Thea said. "What about the Science Officer?"

"That would be Ulrick," Alice said. "He's a Reader, but he comes from a very poor family. Like Kroft, he was also born and raised on Earth. He has no brothers and sisters, but he has a large extended family on Earth, Lunar City, and Anteros. I still can't find a link between the two of you. His family is extremely politically motivated, but yours has nothing they'd want."

"But if Thea's family had a political advantage they wanted, they'd pressure her into marriage, not try to kill her," Beatrice said.

Thea shifted uncomfortably in her chair.

"How about Navigation?" she asked, trying to change the conversation.

"That'd be Quincy," Alice said. "He's an Original, and he basically hates everybody."

"But I met him!" Thea said. "He was perfectly polite."

"Oh yes, he's polite," Alice said. "But if you pay attention, you'll notice he never socializes with any of the other crew members and doesn't associate with any of the passengers, either."

"Well, there is that story of that Original going crazy and killing a bunch of Askovs in Lunar City," Thea said.

"Yes, but that was an isolated case," Beatrice said, waving a hand dismissively. "Quincy doesn't strike me that way at all. Also, he'd gain nothing monetarily or politically."

"Okay, let's continue," Thea said. "What do you know about Operations?"

"That's Rogers," Beatrice said. "He's the only member of the captain's crew that I actually enjoy spending time with. Rogers is jovial, spontaneous, and fun. Occasionally, the crew throws little get-togethers, and he's always at the heart of planning and organizing activities. I can't even imagine him harming anybody. He's Askov, but with no abilities. His family are Viewers, and they're wealthy but have no political connections. Your family has none either, so they'd gain nothing from attacking you. I just can't see any sort of motive for him to harm you."

"Oh, then there's Sam Gotham," Thea said. "Isn't he the head of Engineering?"

"Yes, of course," Alice said. "I didn't think about him because even though he and Lottie aren't speaking to you, he still has no motive to harm you. You already know they're Askov with no abilities. Your families have no financial or political ties. There's no reason for him to harm you."

Thea sighed.

"Now, don't give up, dear," Beatrice said. "We're going to keep looking."

"I know," Thea said with a frown. "I just feel like...I feel as if I'm trying to figure out a puzzle while looking through a thick haze, and I just can't see all the pieces. Like something important is right in front of me, but I can't make it out."

CHAPTER 20

Thea woke up earlier than usual the next morning, disturbed by the thought that somebody had tried to kill her twice. She considered talking to Jemma, who remained her only friend close to her age. But something about talking to Jemma made her uncomfortable. Maybe it was that she was so easily swayed by Lottie and Sam.

"Where are Fiona and Dessie?" Thea asked, pulling on a powder-blue, form-fitted athletic outfit.

"Fiona Young and Desdemona Nicholson are on the Pool and Exercise Deck," the cabin's AI said.

"Are they swimming?" Thea asked, hoping to join them in the pool.

"No. Both women are on the walk-a-tron." the AI said. The walk-a-tron was a raised platform with a moving surface that facilitated walking or running.

A moment later, Thea sighed as she strode out of her cabin, a little disappointed the ladies weren't swimming, but she could always go by herself later. She took the antigrav lift to the Pool and Exercise deck. Once the door opened, she stepped onto a broad walkway that featured numerous workout equipment, personal trainers, and day spas to the left. She was interested in getting a little more information from the older women, who were a fountain of information or gossip.

"Fiona. Dessie," Thea said with a broad smile. "I didn't expect to see you here." She hoped they wouldn't discover her lie.

"Come and join us," Fiona said, waving her over to the walk-a-tron. "We've been discussing poor Imogen and wondering who we should send our condolences to."

"Oh, I thought you were getting some exercise," Thea said with a lopsided smile.

"We really come here to chat," Dessie said, chuckling. She wore green workout clothes that hugged her bony frame.

"*You* come here to chat," Fiona said, putting her hands on her curvy hips. The older woman wore a matching lavender top and bottom. "I come here to walk and maybe lose a couple of kilos."

"So, what were you discussing?" Thea asked, hesitantly stepping onto the raised platform. The walking loop allowed the passengers to see a wonderful view of the stars while they walked, jogged, or ran.

"Well, you know the issue: Imogen cut off her cousins," Dessie said with a frown. "So, do we send condolences to them?"

Fiona and Dessie continued their gentle amble along the moving floor while Thea followed just behind.

"I thought Sam and Jemma were also related to Imogen," Thea said.

"Oh yes," Fiona said with a lopsided smile. "We sent them our sympathies already. But the cousins...would it be against Imogen's wishes to acknowledge them?"

"We have to strike the right balance," Dessie said. "If we appear too friendly, others may think we disagreed with Imogen."

"Who are 'others?'" Thea asked.

"The remaining Stones who agreed with Imogen," Fiona said. "We don't want to offend them, either."

"Oh, I see," Thea said, although she really didn't care. Instead, she changed the subject. "I actually intended to look into Imogen's inheritance more carefully. She's the only victim who could pass on substantial wealth. But then, ironically, nobody can inherit from her."

"Yes, it's all so disconcerting," Fiona said, panting lightly.

"I heard that, too," Dessie said. "I wonder what the attorneys will do?"

A moment of silence passed between the three ladies.

"I dearly miss her," Fiona said in a tremulous voice.

"So do I. She told the best stories," Dessie said. "Do you remember that one about the cousins who got away with stealing slices of cake when they were very little?" She turned to Thea. "Even though they were four or five, they managed to create a diversion, forcing their parents to leave the room and rescue another child. This allowed the ones left in the room to make off with nearly half of the cake."

Fiona and Dessie chuckled.

"That sounds like a sweet story," Thea said. "Creating a diversion is a pretty advanced trick, especially for little kids."

"Yes, it was advanced," Dessie said, but her face fell. "It also foreshadowed what came later. Those were the same cousins who bullied many Askovs and Originals, eventually leading to Imogen disowning them."

"It's funny how past behavior can be an indicator of future character," Thea said.

"It's more like very poor parenting creates criminal adults," Fiona said, pursing her lips.

"That'd explain why they paid for the victims to get medical care instead of punishing their kids," Dessie said

Thea pondered the Stones again, wondering how they could be involved.

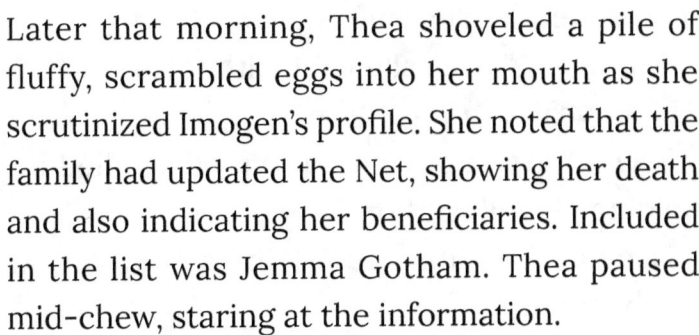

Later that morning, Thea shoveled a pile of fluffy, scrambled eggs into her mouth as she scrutinized Imogen's profile. She noted that the family had updated the Net, showing her death and also indicating her beneficiaries. Included in the list was Jemma Gotham. Thea paused mid-chew, staring at the information.

Didn't Fiona say Jemma wouldn't be able to inherit? she thought.

Wills were public property, but an Askov family could choose to make it private. In fact, most Askovs kept their wills private, but that didn't prevent rumors from disclosing the contents, anyway.

Thea searched for Imogen's will and found an overly simplified version of it. The will dispersed a few trinkets to some close friends, but the majority of her wealth was transferred to Jemma Gotham.

She looked at the date of the Net article, and it was less than an hour old. Even though she had been hesitant to contact Jemma, she realized she needed more information. She sent Jemma a quick note, and then she finished the last of her breakfast. Changing into a comfortable, dusty pink dress, she waited for Jemma. A moment later, the doorbell chimed.

"Come in," Thea called out without asking the AI to reveal who was there.

The door slid open, and Jemma strolled in, holding a small flat box.

"I come bearing gifts," Jemma said with a bright smile.

"Oh really? What are those?" Thea asked, grinning despite her mild unease around Jemma.

She placed the box on the coffee table between them and then took a seat in one of the overstuffed chairs while Thea sat opposite on the sofa.

"These are Anteros Flower Buns," Jemma said with a broad grin. "My grandmother created this recipe when meal crafters were still new and not very good."

Thea tried her best to maintain her smile because Anteros pastries were known to be horrendously tough or leathery. She couldn't tolerate them any longer, especially after she'd spent years on Earth eating pastries from a medley of cafés and restaurants all over Tymal and Heliton.

"I know what you're thinking," Jemma said with a chuckle. "You're assuming this will have the texture of a stone or a hard puck from Space Puck. But I promise my grandmother had a very good recipe, and I think you'll really like this."

Thea selected a button on the crafter, and two small plates, each with a knife and fork, appeared in front of each of them. Jemma picked up something that looked like a soft, overfilled bun and gently pulled it apart.

A soft, thick, reddish, sweet-smelling liquid squeezed from the middle of the pastry, and she quickly placed half a roll on each plate.

"This pastry has won many awards in Anteros," Jemma said with a bit of pride in her voice.

Thea picked up her knife and fork and gently sliced into a tiny corner of the flower pastry.

"Well, it's soft...that's good," Thea said, stabbing the tiny piece with her fork. She lifted it to her nose and inhaled the wonderful aromatic scent before gently placing it in her mouth. It was like a flavor bomb went off in her mouth. The smell was strong but pleasant. The taste was delicate and intricate. However, the mismatch between the strong smell and gentle flavor worked.

"This is amazing," Thea said after she swallowed. "Why haven't I had this before?"

"I don't know why my mom always kept it a secret," Jemma said, popping a large mouthful into her mouth.

In a few seconds, the two ladies finished their halves of the first flower pastry, and both eyed the remaining one in the box.

"Want to split that one, too?" Jemma asked with a sly smile.

Thea enthusiastically nodded.

They ate the remaining pastry and ended with a hot cup of tea.

"That was amazing. Thank you for the pastry," Thea said. "I can't believe I lived in Anteros my whole life and never tasted those buns."

"Well, very few people have," Jemma said, shaking her head. "My mom was very particular about who she'd share them with, but she passed away about a year ago, and she willed the recipe onto me."

"Oh, only a year ago?" Thea said with a small frown. "I'm sorry to hear that."

"Oh, it's okay. It doesn't hurt as much now, but I still miss her every day."

"Would you mind if I ask you some questions about your family?" Thea said gently.

"Of course not," Jemma said. "What do you want to know?"

"Has your dad passed away, too?" Thea asked.

"Yes, it's just Sam and me now," Jemma said, wiping at the crumbs on the table and placing everything into the recycling.

"Well, I just read Imogen's will," Thea said, glancing at the ceiling. "I mean a summary of her will. It seems she left almost everything to you. I'm just confused because I thought you couldn't inherit from her."

"What!" Jemma said with raised eyebrows. "How could I inherit it? I'm barely a Reader. I've had very little training."

"The information on the Net is about an hour old," Thea said. "You had no idea?"

Jemma shook her head with worry etched on her face.

"I understand the terms of Imogen's inheritance were that the beneficiary had to be a fully trained Askovian," Thea said. "But I thought you said you also went to Heliton?"

"Well, just for a year," Jemma said. "It was actually Aunt who suggested it. She said that even if my abilities were weak, a little bit of training might help. And she turned out to be right. Before, I could never control anything, and afterward, I could do small things."

"You said Imogen suggested it?"

"Oh yes, she put a bit of pressure on Mom and Dad to make sure I got some training. But like I said, it wasn't very much, and it was years ago."

"I wonder if she was preparing for this day. The will is pretty clear that you inherit."

"Wait a minute, you're asking me questions?" Jemma's eyes bored into Thea's. "Am I a suspect?"

"Actually, I don't think you're capable of murdering your aunt," Thea said, tilting her head. "You loved her. But when I think this through logically, the only person who benefits from Imogen's death is you." She sighed. "Did you ever hear that story Imogen told about the cousins who stole when they were kids..."

"Yes, yes, I heard that one a million times," Jemma said, waving a hand dismissively. "She felt they were so cute because together, they organized, distracted their parents, and stole some food or some nonsense like that."

"Yes, something like that," Thea said, wondering at Jemma's irritation.

"Aunt saw it as cute," Jemma said. "I saw it as training future bullies. Well, I'm glad they didn't inherit anything, and I don't care if that makes me sound guilty. They were horrible, horrible people."

"What I don't understand is why you didn't know you had inherited," Thea said. "They should've contacted you before making the will public."

"Yes, that's right," Jemma said. "I didn't think about that. That's a very basic mistake for an attorney to make."

"Do you think Sam knows anything about this?" Thea asked in a steady voice, peering at Jemma. The door to the cabin slid open while Thea and Jemma turned to see Sam framed by the doorway with a scowl on his face.

CHAPTER 21

Sam still wore his dark blue crew uniform as he stalked into the room. A shiver ran down Thea's spine; she'd hoped for more time to speak with Jemma.

"Sam, what are you doing here?" Jemma said, eyebrows raised.

"I might ask you the same thing," Sam said in a harsh voice. "Don't you know what she's doing? She's trying to squeeze information out of you so she can frame me for murder."

"You must be joking," Jemma said, chuckling.

"You've been listening to our conversation?" Thea asked with furrowed eyebrows. "How?"

"No, Sam would never do that," Jemma said. "I mean, he's not even on our suspect list."

"Actually, that's not true," Thea said in a level voice. "I began suspecting Sam after the IPS released Alice. But I couldn't figure out a real

motive until I discovered you were the beneficiary of Imogen's will."

"You see?" Sam barked. "It's just like I told you.
She's trying to frame me just because I'm one of
six people who have enough command permissions to have carried out the attacks. If she tells
anyone, it won't matter if I say I'm innocent."

"Why would he do it?" Jemma asked as the
smile fell from her face, and she turned to Thea.
"Sam gains nothing from Aunt's death."

"Are you sure about that?" Thea asked. "If
you became wealthy and Sam asked for an al-
lowance, would you actually say no?"

Jemma hesitated, clearing her throat.

"Don't fall for it, Jemma," Sam said, drawing
his lips in a straight line. "She's just trying to
force a wedge between us. I had no reason to
harm Thea or Veronica. Obviously, I'm not the
murderer."

"That's a good point," Jemma said, nodding.
"Why would he kill Veronica? Also, he didn't
even know you before the trip."

"I've been considering that," Thea said. "You
know what eventually made me think different-
ly? That cute story from Imogen about how the
toddlers created a diversion and managed to

steal slices of cake. What do Veronica, Imogen, and I have in common?"

"Well, you're all Askovians," Jemma said.

"Oh sure, we are," Thea said, narrowing her eyes. "But there are plenty of Askovians on this ship. Why us? It's because Veronica and I were both estranged from our families. Imogen's heirs didn't really care for her, but they'd be happy to benefit from the inheritance. Owen could've tried to force an investigation into Veronica's death, but the IPS detained him twice. I don't think he would've done anything. You see, there was no one left to fight for us."

Jemma peered down at the table in contemplation.

"This is misdirection," Sam said, stomping further into the room. "I think you're trying to cover something up. Why is it that the murderer managed to actually kill Veronica and Imogen but somehow missed murdering you? Were you ever really in danger?"

Jemma gasped, eyes wide as she turned to Thea.

There it was...Jemma's fundamental lack of trust. She congratulated herself on remaining wary of Jemma, but that meant now she was in danger.

"Good point," Thea said slowly, rising to her feet. She kept her panic in check while trying to think of an escape. Stepping casually around the back of the sofa, she tried to put some distance between her and Sam. "If I had wanted to divert attention away from myself, I could've made myself another victim. The only problem is I don't have any command permissions."

"But you majored in engineering," Sam said, crossing his arms, his eyes staring daggers at her. "You could've hacked into our system, taking control of one of our system processes."

"Is that what you think?" Thea said with a half-smile. His words were for Jemma's benefit; as an engineer, he knew better. "Life's not like those entertainment serials. Nobody can just hack into an AI's system. It takes very advanced programming skills, which I don't have."

"But when you think about it, a Mover could've accomplished both murders," Jemma said, taking a small step away from her chair and closer to her brother. "I don't know about the command access, but I know either a robot or a Mover could've thrown Veronica down that shaft. Also, suffocating Imogen could have happened before the Fire System removed the oxygen from the room. I know a Mover can surround another person with a small air pocket, suffocating them."

"You've been watching too many serials also," Thea said, openly laughing. "I definitely encountered advanced Movers like that when I was at Heliton, but they were the minority. I'm just a run-of-the-mill Mover who can manipulate medium to large objects. Those micro-Movers are rare."

Jemma studied her face as if confused, but Thea expected Jemma to continue to support her brother.

"What I want to know is why Sam needed Veronica, Imogen, and me to suffer," Thea said, her eyes boring into Sam's. "You made sure Veronica suffered the fall down the antigrav shaft. You also allowed Imogen to suffocate to death. Also, even though I lived, the poison created excruciating pain, and the time in the airlock...it still gives me nightmares."

"Don't believe a word she says, Jemma," Sam said, glaring at Thea. "I didn't do anything to anybody. If any of them were in pain, it wasn't my fault. She's trying to pin this murder on me because a lot of the evidence points toward her."

Jemma turned, gazing at her brother's stoic face and then back again at Thea's. "I've encountered a lot of Askovians, who were basically power-hungry thugs. They start that way as kids, and even as adults, that part of their personality didn't go away. Even though I can't imagine you killing anybody, Sam isn't wrong."

Sam smirked and took several steps to stand beside his sister. Thea shuddered, realizing she was in real danger, and stepped away from the sofa, ending with her back against a wall. Her Mover abilities might save her, but manipulating both Sam and Jemma would be beyond her capabilities. She had to be smart.

"Jemma, think about this in terms of distraction," Thea said, trying to keep the panic out of her voice. "Imagine what would've happened if only Imogen died with you as the only beneficiary. You would have been their prime suspect." She paused, examining Jemma with a tiny hope she'd see Sam's guilt. "Since Sam killed Veronica and attacked me when the IPS investigated Imogen's murder, they had to include all three victims. They'd never put all of their energy into focusing only on Imogen because the attacks appear linked. Now there's a lot of confusion, and the result is the IPS investigation has no real suspects."

Jemma glanced at her brother, confusion etched on her face.

"Don't listen to her," Sam said, as his face tightened. "She's just trying to confuse you. As an engineer, she could've arranged to have Veronica and Imogen murdered while making herself look like an innocent victim. She's an advanced programmer, and there's no way to check because people with those skills don't usually acquire them in school—they learn the skills through black market dealings."

"What Sam says makes sense," Jemma frowned, turning to Thea with a sorrowful face.

Thea's stomach sank, knowing she was completely on her own, but she had a plan. Centering herself like she'd learned in school, she focused all of her energy on Sam. A moment later, she deliberately pushed him hard enough to knock Jemma over and slam him against a distant wall. Thea then raced around the sofa, past Jemma, who lay on the floor, and she nearly collided with her cabin door.

First, she used her abilities to pull the door about, but a tightness formed in her chest with her rising panic. Next, she scratched at the line between the door and wall, trying to pry it open, but it wouldn't budge. Frantically pressing a button on her comm, she shifted from foot-to-foot, but the door remained stuck. In fact, her bracelet had turned dark—completely disabled. Lunging at the door again, she kept scratching at the opening when she heard slow laughter building behind her. Turning, she watched Sam limp toward his sister and help her onto a chair. She was awake but clearly still groggy.

He turned to face Thea as his laughter filled the room. Thea trembled as her blood turned cold.

CHAPTER 22

Thea wracked her brain. This was just like being trapped in the airlock again. The only problem was this time, there was no other way to sound the alarm. She needed to at least see what she could manipulate before using her Mover abilities. She tried manipulating the fire system for her cabin using her memory of the fire system in Imogen's cabin. Nothing happened; Sam had clearly disabled it. Then she tried activating the general alarm for her cabin again—nothing.

She wondered if the pantry system had any sort of alarm when she gasped. The pantry system is large enough to allow a robot to step behind it for repairs, and they're connected to all the nearby cabins. Her cabin was at the end of a row of quarters, and she wondered how far she'd need to go for help. At the moment, though, her main concern was getting away from Sam.

After he'd helped his sister into a chair, he turned toward Thea and pressed a button on his comm. A second later, the door to her cabin opened.

Thea immediately spun around to sprint out of the cabin. She froze as she took in the sight of the same shiny gray metal robot that had captured her a few nights ago and placed her in the airlock. With lightning speed, it reached out and grasped both of her arms. Thea screamed as the robot raised her off the floor while she kicked at its legs.

Stepping into the room, the door sealed as the robot rotated her body to carry her like it had the night of her abduction. It supported her on her back and knees while maintaining a tight grip. Stepping behind the sofa, it lowered her onto the seat, pinning her arms to her side.

"Sam, what are you doing?" Jemma asked in a groggy voice. "Please don't hurt her. Even if she's the murderer, we should leave this to the IPS."

"The IPS is useless." Sam scoffed. "We need to take care of her ourselves."

"Take care of her?" Jemma asked, shaking her head. "I don't like where you're going with this, Sam. I agree she's most likely guilty, but I don't agree with killing her."

"Jemma, use your brain!" Thea yelled at her. "He needs to kill me because I can prove he did it."

Jemma and Sam both turned to her with different degrees of shock on their faces. "Are you saying you have proof?" Jemma asked, both eyebrows raised.

"Yes," Thea said, trying to keep her voice steady.

"She's lying," Sam said, his face contorted in rage. "If she had proof, she would've turned it into the IPS by now."

"Y-Yes," Jemma said hesitantly. "But if she doesn't have proof, then we should just turn her into the IPS."

"I said no," Sam said in a gruff voice. "If she has a chance to talk to the IPS, it'll muddy the waters of their investigation, and then nobody will pay for Imogen's murder. We owe this to Imogen."

Jemma wrung her hands together, wavering again. "What about Lottie?" Jemma asked. "We should ask her for her input, too. She might have other ideas that could help us."

"Definitely not," Sam said, almost growling at her. "The fewer people who know about this, the safer we'll all be."

During their discussion, Thea struggled to remember how this class of robot had been constructed. Her family's farm used a similar model, and their CPU was maintained in the abdominal cavity, the most reinforced portion of the entire robot. The head, arms, and legs were interchangeable appendages to adapt to the needs of the owner. She carefully used her abilities to poke the sides of the robot. Constructed with a sturdy frame, brute force was not going to work. Instead, she needed to gently test the resistance around the robot's abdomen to find any weak spots. It was a clever construction. The torso consisted of a chest and abdomen. Armor plates protected the chest, which concealed the entrance to the abdominal area. *There it is*, she thought as she repressed a sigh of relief. The abdomen's top contained the only unreinforced spot.

Centering herself, Thea focused only on the weak portion under the armor. She applied all of her strength and punched through the weak abdominal top, straight through what felt like quite a few electronics all the way to the bottom of the cavity. It wasn't obvious at first, but Thea suspected the robot had failed in its current position, leaning halfway over her with its hands clamped around her arms.

When Sam and Jemma weren't looking, she used her abilities to pry the robot's hands slightly away from her right arm and then from her left. Glancing at the pantry, she wondered how she could get behind it. She'd never worked any of the controls to open it, trusting that the Operations department would keep her pantry automatically stocked. She wondered if she'd have to use brute force, but then that'd allow Sam to follow her. Unexpectedly, Sam turned toward her, and she jumped.

"Are you afraid of me?" Sam said as a menacing smile covered his face. "You should be." He glanced at Jemma, and worry crossed his face. "There's an IPS meeting I can't skip without drawing attention."

"What's the matter?" Jemma asked.

"I just don't think I can trust you not to free her," Sam said. "You have to come with me, and I'll lock her in here. She won't be able to get out."

"Sam, I really disagree with this," Jemma said. "Let me come with you to the meeting with the IPS, and let's explain this together."

"No!" Sam yelled, his face contorted with rage. "I knew I couldn't leave you alone with her. If you come with me, the robot will keep her on that sofa. We can talk on the way to your cabin." He activated his comm, the doors to Thea's cabin opened, and they left.

Thea waited a couple of minutes, hoping it wasn't a trick. She worried there was no meeting, and instead, Sam simply needed Jemma out of the room so he could kill her. Removing her arms from the robot's grasp, she carefully stood and gazed at the immobile robot. Then she raced to the cabin door, but it wouldn't open, as she expected. Next, she dashed to the back of the dining room, where she assumed the pantry door would be. Selecting a number of spaces along the wall, she frantically looked for some button that might open the pantry door, like the buttons around the airlock. When that didn't work, she turned to the meal crafter and wondered if that was the real entrance. She'd never used the crafter in that way, but she didn't have much time.

Taking two giant steps to the dining room table, she searched through the menu options on the crafter when she finally saw it—Pantry Door. After she made her selection, a disguised door suddenly slid open at the back of the room, and relief flooded Thea's body. *I might actually get out of this nightmare alive.*

She raced through the door and squeezed into a narrow corridor intended for maintenance robots. For a second, the cool, refrigerated air shocked her, but it kept the food items preserved. She found the pantry door's controls on the adjacent wall. Then she closed and locked it. There wasn't much room back there, but she could move as long as she stayed sideways. To her left were hundreds of clear containers stacked from floor to ceiling, each containing powdered food. Further left was a meal processor that extracted the foods required for her requested meals.

After glancing at the pantry, she turned her head to the right and pressed her body along the narrow space in the direction of the neighboring cabin. She didn't know the occupant of this cabin, but she knew Beatrice's cabin was just three pantry stops away. She continued shuffling forward as goosebumps rose on her skin from the cool refrigerated air. Suddenly, she heard another door open in the direction of her cabin.

"Get back here!" Sam yelled. "I don't even know how you got in here. Why did you run? Was it that obvious I had to kill you when Jemma wasn't around?"

Panic flooded Thea's body as she squeezed into the next cabin's pantry. Instead of waiting for Beatrice's cabin, she selected the pantry door controls for this cabin. What she hadn't counted on was the tiny finger scanner on each button. Probably the cabin's occupants or someone with command permissions could operate these doors, but they refused to budge for her. Sweat beaded on her forehead as she realized she was stuck.

"Help! Help!" Thea cried, banging on the door. "I'm stuck back here! Open the pantry!"

When she didn't hear anything, she continued scooting along the corridor.

"Quiet! Keep it down!" Sam roared as he grunted. He was thicker than Thea and clearly struggled to maneuver in the same space. When Thea reached the next cabin, she selected the pantry door button, but it didn't work as well. Finally, she banged on it, shouting for help again.

"Would you shut up?" Sam bellowed, groaning as his clothing got stuck on the previous cabin's pantry. Thea gasped as she realized how close he'd gotten. Without calming her mind or centering her focus, she used her Mover abilities to push him back toward her cabin.

"Argh!" Sam yelled. "Stop it. You're just making this harder."

Unfortunately, Sam didn't move toward her cabin, but he also didn't move any closer to her.

She scooted further along the narrow corridor and banged on the third cabin's door.

"Help! Help!" she screamed. "I'm stuck back here!"

This time, Sam didn't yell but huffed in and out as he labored to catch up with her. Suddenly, a whooshing sound interrupted them.

"Thea? Is that you?" Beatrice asked, framed by the open pantry door. "What are you doing back here?"

"Sam Gotham is trying to kill me!" Thea shouted as she tumbled through the door. "Call the IPS now!"

CHAPTER 23

After Thea stumbled through the pantry door, she found herself in Beatrice's quarters. The older woman guided her away from the pantry door to the dining room table.

"We need to get help!" Thea said in a strained voice.

"Come and have a seat," Beatrice said, pulling out a chair. "I called the IPS when I first heard you in that pantry corridor."

Agent Clark raced into the cabin toward Thea and Beatrice. She dashed behind the two ladies, heading for her pantry door. A moment later, she squeezed herself inside and disappeared.

"I hope there's another agent," Thea said, staring at the opening in the wall.

"They have Sam cornered," Beatrice asked, rubbing Thea's hand. "The ship's AI explained what would happen and asked me to wait for you." She paused, peering carefully at Thea. "Are you hurt?"

"No," Thea said, trembling. "But what if Sam escapes?"

"From two fully trained IPS agents?" Beatrice scoffed. "You're perfectly safe."

Several minutes later, Agents Clark and Walker squeezed through the pantry door into the dining room. They each held one of Sam's arms as he struggled to break free.

"Samuel Gotham, you are under arrest," Agent Walker said in a commanding voice.

"No, no!" Sam shouted, his face ashen. "It's not me, it's that Askovian. She's manipulating you." He glared at Thea. Their shouting match went on for several minutes before the IPS agents forced him out of Beatrice's cabin.

Thea sat at Beatrice's dining room table, shaking. Her mind whirled with the events of the past hour and how close she'd come to death.

"My mother always swore by hot tea to cure any upset," Beatrice said in a gentle voice while making a selection on the meal crafter.

A moment later, a steaming cup appeared on the table. Thea took a sip, letting the warm liquid flow into her stomach; the warmth helped to relax her.

"Is that better?" Beatrice asked.

"Yes," Thea said with a small smile. Even though Beatrice treated her like a small child, Thea found it comforting. "I can't believe he murdered two women and then tried to murder me three times. Even though I understand why he did it, some part of me just can't accept it. This was just for some credits!"

"Well, when you're as old as I am, the behavior of truly wicked people doesn't surprise you as much," Beatrice said. "Given the wealth that Jemma stood to inherit, it's not surprising to me at all that he decided murdering two women was a good idea."

"I hope I'm not too late," Dr. Hadley said, entering the cabin holding a small navy blue bag that matched her uniform. "I just got the notification from the IPS."

"You're not late at all," Beatrice said. "In fact, I'd say you're right on time."

Dr. Hadley removed a hand scanner from her bag and slowly traced it over Thea's body. A floating screen appeared over Dr. Hadley's wrist, and as she examined the contents of the hand scanner, which were now displayed on the floating screen, her eyebrows wrinkled for just a moment before her face brightened.

"Well, except for maybe a few scratches and bruises, you're okay," Dr. Hadley said. "How are you feeling?"

"Shaken. Scared. Shocked." Thea took a steadying breath. "My brain is still struggling to put all the pieces together."

"Would you tell me exactly what happened?" Dr. Hadley asked.

"It's so dark and sordid," Thea said quietly. "It would've taken Sam months to plan." She swallowed some tea and sighed. "Around fifteen years ago, Imogen and Jemma's parents had many discussions about their daughter's future. Imogen had always been close to Jemma, who wanted to go to Heliton to learn more about her abilities. But because her Reader abilities were so weak, her parents didn't think it was worth it to train her. Imogen continued talking to them, and in the end, her parents sent Jemma to Heliton. She was only there for a year; it was all they could afford. Unexpectedly, this made Jemma qualified to receive an inheritance from Imogen."

"But why kill Veronica or try to kill you?" Dr. Hadley asked.

"I'll get to that in a minute," Thea said, taking another sip of hot tea. "Now, about two years ago, Imogen discovered that her cousins had been systematically harassing and attacking other Askovs and Originals also around fifteen years ago. She also found that their parents had been covering it up. She was so disgusted she wanted to punish them."

"That's when she changed her will," Beatrice said. "We were all with her on Earth when she did it."

"Exactly," Thea said. "After the change, only Jemma could inherit. Also, that process took several months of the attorneys' careful rearrangement because of the specific terms of the will, and only recently did they complete the new will."

"Whose idea was it to make the journey back to Anteros?" Dr. Hadley asked.

"Everyone's," Beatrice said. "Every two to three years, Imogen and the rest of us travel between Mars and Earth."

"So you all made plans to head back to Anteros just as Imogen's new will went into effect?" Dr. Hadley asked.

"It was the perfect time for Sam to strike," Thea said, frowning. "There aren't that many ships that travel between the two planets, and Sam is a trusted crew member. When you all boarded the Stargazer, Sam set his plan in motion. Killing Veronica and me would provide a diversion, and there would be no families to demand an investigation. Veronica had been disowned, and Owen was actually a suspect fighting for his own freedom. My family disowned me as well, but Sam got unlucky, and I survived. But that didn't slow him down. I'm sure he felt that because of the attempt on my life, the IPS would still link my attack to Veronica's death. Of course, his intended victim was—"

"Imogen," Beatrice said in a quiet voice.

Thea nodded.

"But the IPS would've figured it out," Dr. Hadley said.

"I don't think so," Thea said with furrowed eyebrows. "From the IPS's point of view, there are now two murders and an attempted murder in a short period of time. They appear connected. Also, remember, Sam framed Alice for the murders. This was just one more thing the IPS needed to analyze."

"I'm glad Imogen never knew about Sam," Beatrice said, shaking her head. "That would've broken her."

"Right now, you're in shock," Dr. Hadley said, eying Thea. "I can give you a sedative to help with that."

Thea shook her head and gulped the last of her tea.

"Thea! Thea!" Alice burst into the room. "I just heard what happened! Are you alright?" She quickly took an empty chair next to Thea.

A gentle smile crossed Thea's face as Alice hugged her. There was something so comforting about having people around her who genuinely cared. Just when she was about to give up on humanity after facing Lottie and Jemma's betrayal, she encountered even more support and friendship from Beatrice and Alice.

"What I don't quite understand is how the IPS got here so quickly," Thea said.

"I heard them talking," Alice said. "Jemma called the IPS after Sam locked her in her cabin and deactivated her comm. You see, Lottie came to visit Jemma. Her bracelet opened Jemma's door, and she immediately escaped her quarters. Once in the walkway, her comm activated again, and she contacted the IPS. It turns out Lottie is still not happy about that, though."

"I also contacted the IPS when I heard you in the corridor," Beatrice said. "Although I suspect it was after Jemma reached them. But it took me a while to figure out how to open the pantry door."

"Well, I'm happy to hear Jemma tried to help," Thea said, scoffing. "But I'm not surprised by Lottie's reaction."

"Isn't that a strange reaction to hearing your husband's a murderer?" Alice asked. "You'd think Lottie'd be shocked or maybe would've even helped Jemma."

"Or maybe Lottie was in on it," Beatrice said with a knowing look.

"Now we can't jump to conclusions," Dr. Hadley said. "On the other hand, I've gotten to know Jemma a little during this trip. She seems to have a lot more integrity than her brother."

"Maybe so," Thea said, staring into her cup. "She argued a little with her brother as she initially tried to defend me. Of course, it didn't work."

For the next few hours, women sat around the dining room table discussing Sam and the murders.

A couple of days later, Thea sat on her sofa, watching an entertainment serial. Even though it was the middle of the afternoon, she still wore her dusty pink pajamas. For the past few days, she'd been hiding from the rest of the world. Her door chimed, interrupting her show, and she glanced in its direction before continuing the drama.

"Agent Walker has requested permission to enter your cabin," the AI said. "It is urgent."

She jolted upright, pulling her feet off the coffee table. She closed the floating screen displaying her serial and dusted crumbs off her pajamas. As she stood, she said, "Open the door."

"May I come in?" Agent Walker asked, standing in the doorway.

"Yes, please," Thea said, hastily brushing at a dried food stain while greeting him in her pajamas.

"I'm so sorry to interrupt," Agent Walker said as he continued into her cabin and grabbed a chair opposite her. He looked the same as always, with his perfectly clipped blond hair and crisp navy blue uniform.

"We've spent the past few days interrogating Sam Gotham," Walker said, rubbing his forehead. "It's been...challenging."

"What do you mean by 'challenging?'" Thea asked.

"Unfortunately, I can't go into it," Walker said as a moment of irritation crossed his face. "However, a few things have come to light. Mr. Gotham has been tracking you since you stepped on board. Do you remember the first time we met?"

"That wasn't Sam, was it?" Thea asked.

"Yes," the agent said. "Either Mr. Gotham or the person who altered your comm bracelet corrupted its functions—it has a fairly subtle flaw. Gotham was able to exploit it immediately and used it to track you everywhere on board the ship. He used it to make it appear that you were in Veronica's cabin when he arranged to murder her. A lot of our investigation connected to any sort of comm signals is completely compromised. He's also been monitoring your conversations."

"That's interesting," Thea said, scratching her head. "You see, I thought he was using Lottie to gather information."

"His fiancée, Ms. Dover, provided some information, and so did his sister, Jemma," Agent Walker said. "But the majority of the information came from your comm."

Thea gazed at her bracelet for several seconds. She remembered the first time she'd received it and how special she felt it was. But it had been bad luck on Anteros, more so on Earth, and now on the Stargazer. *I should've gotten a new comm,* she thought as a wave of regret washed over her.

"Based on what we've discovered, Mr. Gotham mostly used his sister and fiancée to distract you," Walker said. "Remember how they mentioned they were going to start their own investigation?"

"Yes, I remember that," Thea said. "At first, I thought it seemed a little silly, but then they appeared to really dive into the investigation. They gathered all the older ladies, and we really talked things through. Was all of that just a distraction?"

"Yes, definitely," Walker said. "Spending so much time on Veronica Dover created a distraction for us, too. There was no way of really knowing that his true intended victim was Imogen Stone."

Thea shivered as she realized the depth of Sam's schemes.

"My recommendation is to change that bracelet as quickly as possible," Walker said.

"Get a temporary one, which is available on the ship for now, and disable the blue-tinted one on your wrist."

"Well, surely I don't need to do anything right away," Thea said, putting a protective arm around the teal comm.

"If Sam Gotham discovered the flaw in that comm, somebody else could as well," the agent said. "Your identity is not safe. You could lose credits, your new job, and your freedom. Remember, he could make you appear someplace you're not—we could've arrested you."

Thea tensed at the last comment—it struck a little too close to home.

"Well, that's all I wanted to say," Walker said, his mouth set in a grim line. "I want to emphasize how very important this is. Please change your bracelet as soon as possible."

Walker stood, and Thea rose a second later. They nodded to each other, and Walker strolled out of the room.

Thea gazed down at her bracelet, unsure of what to do.

CHAPTER 24

Later that evening, Thea sat in Alice's cabin surrounded by her new friends. She had showered and wore a casual tan top with matching pants. Lounging on the sofa and surrounded by chatter, she lightly followed the conversation.

Beatrice and Alice also reclined in overstuffed chairs with their feet on the coffee table. Earlier, Thea told them about her visit with Agent Walker.

"I'm astounded at the level of work that went into that plan," Beatrice said with raised eyebrows.

"Stalking you? The whole time?" Alice asked. "I can barely believe it."

"So, when are you going to change that comm?" Beatrice asked, eying it with narrowed eyes.

"That's the problem," Thea said with a heavy sigh. "It has sentimental value."

"What?" Alice said a little louder. "He tried to kill you with that thing. What could be more important than your life?"

"Now, now," Beatrice said in a gentle voice. "Calm down. Let her tell us about the comm."

Thea surveyed the bracelet as Alice's words replayed in her mind.

"My first love gave it to me." Thea spoke softly. "I know it's silly. Well...dangerous, but I can't seem to let go of it."

"Is this the reason you changed your last name?" Beatrice asked. "Didn't your family approve?"

Thea sighed and focused on the coffee table for a moment before turning back to both ladies.

"In my family, let's just say I'm not as *treasured* as my older siblings. They both could choose their spouses and generally had more control over their lives. I was in love with and ready to marry Evan. It would've been the two of us against our families." A dry laugh escaped her lips.

"Things didn't go the way you imagined?" Alice asked.

"No," Thea said, taking a deep breath. "Evan's parents bribed him with more credits than either of us had ever seen. Within twenty-four hours, he married their choice for him, and he disappeared from my life."

"I'm so sorry," Beatrice said. "But if he left you, why are you still hanging on the comm?"

"I don't know." Thea chuckled. "I'm not making sense."

"Are you still hoping there's a chance you'll get back together?" Alice asked.

"No," Thea said and remained quiet for several minutes. "I can't imagine that after Evan, I'll ever feel like that about someone else."

Beatrice and Alice tittered.

"Not only will you feel that way again," Alice said. "You'll probably feel that way about several more men."

Thea frowned, not believing a word they said.

"So, you haven't told us why you changed your name," Beatrice said.

"Yes, well..." Thea said. "After I lost Evan, I had to get away. I basically made a deal with my parents. I agreed to become betrothed to one of the Chapman family members. They didn't tell me who, and I assumed it was going to be the youngest. I moved to Earth and enrolled in

Heliton. But a couple of years after I arrived, the Chapmans stopped communicating with me or my parents. There was a formal contract in place, and if they didn't marry into our family, my parents would've sued."

"Was this a credits issue?" Alice asked with one raised eyebrow.

"Absolutely!" Thea said. "The farming industry fluctuates wildly, depending on who enters the market and who goes bankrupt. Nowadays, there are more farmers than mouths to feed, but during the initial Mars colonization, it was the most lucrative business to get into."

"They must have put a lot of pressure on you to marry," Beatrice said in a sympathetic voice.

"Yes," Thea said, barely getting the words out as she fought the sob that threatened to escape. She continued after a moment. "I agreed to go along with my parents' choice. I'm a Mover and can bring a small amount of prestige to the Chapman family, whereas my family needed the credits. I finally contacted the Chapman's directly and discovered my intended partner was already married, and they were in a full panic to fix things."

"That must've been unexpected," Alice said.

"I didn't mind at all," Thea said, chuckling. "The marriage couldn't take place, so I needed a plan. I prepared for my future by securing a job at Brimble Mining on Ganymede. They want to establish a new independent farm to save credits by not needing to transport food items from Anteros. Romlys are farmers, and also it's what I'd studied at Heliton. The job was perfectly suited for me. I explained everything to my parents, but they reminded me that I'd signed the marriage contract. Also, I needed to remain on Earth while they proceeded with legal action."

"But were you an adult?" Beatrice asked.

"Yes," Thea said, nodding. "I was legally an adult when I signed it. My parents didn't really care if I married or not, they just wanted the credits due since the Chapmans didn't stick to the contract. I never wanted to marry so...I ran away."

"That's when you changed your name from Romly to Black," Alice said, like a statement instead of a question.

"I thought that by leaving Earth, I'd be safe from my parents," Thea said. "In any case, the Chapmans would be relieved that I'd technically broken the agreement by leaving." Thea sighed.

"But my new job is on Ganymede, and the only way to get there is through Anteros. My plan was to stay away from Askovs on the Stargazer, but I miscalculated. Sam figured out who I was, told his sister, and she told the rest of you. Sometimes I think I should've just stayed on Earth and let my parents sue the Chapmans while they chose another husband for me. I don't know."

Beatrice and Alice remained silent for a while. Thea stared down at the coffee table, lost in thought.

"I know you spoke to Captain Ebert," Beatrice said. "Did he have any advice?"

"He promised to help if I ran into trouble," Thea said. "But otherwise, he didn't offer any guidance."

"Legally, your parents are in the right," Alice said, worry etched in her voice. "If they're as desperate as you say, this won't go well. What are you going to do when we arrive? There's only one official exit off this ship."

"I don't know," Thea said in a sad voice. "I suppose I have seven months to come up with something. But knowing my family, they're not going to let this go. They absolutely won't allow me to continue to Ganymede. But no matter what they do, they absolutely can't force me to marry."

***

To enjoy more cozy mystery science fiction, pick up The Puzzle Safe Mystery (https://katherinesbooks.com/psmamz/).

PLEASE LEAVE AN HONEST REVIEW

Authors thrive on reviews. These reviews help other readers decide whether to buy the book. To write a review, simply provide a star rating and add a couple of sentences explaining why you liked the book. Thank you for your review. Click on the link below to leave a review.

https://katherinesbooks.com/runawaymartianreviewamz

WOULD YOU LIKE ANOTHER SCI-FI WHODUNIT?

Want to know how it all began? Dive into *Short Stories from the Feeler Universe* (https://katherinesbooks.com/sci-fi-short-story/), and once you join my newsletter, read this thrilling short story from *The Feeler* series! This prequel takes you to the very beginning, where Cora uses her unique Feeler abilities to unravel a gripping whodunit.

Books

Standalone Books

The Puzzle Safe Mystery
https://katherinesbooks.com/psmamz
The Runaway Martian
https://katherinesbooks.com/runawaymartia
namz
***

The Feeler Series Books

The Feeler (Book 1)
katherinesbooks.com/feeler
Movers, Mines, and Murder (Book 2)
katherinesbooks.com/movers
Lunar Justice (Book 3)
katherinesbooks.com/lunarjustice
Spencer Legacy (Book 4)

katherinesbooks.com/spencerlegacy

ABOUT THE AUTHOR

Katherine is a science fiction author who spent nearly thirty years working as an engineer before retiring and turning to her life-long love of storytelling. She grew up devouring classic sci-fi, especially the works of Isaac Asimov, Arthur C. Clarke, and Ray Bradbury. As much as she adored those stories, she often felt something was missing.

Over time, her reading tastes broadened to include cozy mysteries, thrillers, and fantasy. Eventually she realized her ideal book would be a blend of the genres she loved most. The solution was obvious: write cross-genre stories that fuse the wonder of science fiction with the charm and puzzle-solving of cozy mystery.

Katherine lives in New England, where she spends her days writing, reading, and enjoying time with her family.